THE KEY TO A MURDER

By John Marvey Murray

GW00400269

The Key to a Murder *by John Harvey Murray*

Chapter 1

Falling accounted for 6,217 out of 530,841 accidental deaths in 2019. This fact always struck me as rather boring, so much so that I never enquired as to the number of non-accidental deaths for which falls were responsible, until the whole subject took on a relevance I had never imagined.

"Murder! You can NOT be serious!" exclaimed Samuel Owain Hoyle, braking far too sharply as we approached a junction on our way back from the rugby ground at Llanrumney. We had been dissecting the match our team had just lost, mainly, in his opinion, due to my poor performance as scrum half. He had rightly deduced that something was troubling me.

"It's true, Esso. I heard only the other day. I find it hard to believe too." Sam's friends called him Esso because he was S O 'Oyle, just as mine called me Charlie because my name is Matthew Chaplain, ignoring the fact that the famous Charlie spelt his name 'Chaplin'. I often wondered if it was a coincidence that there had been lots of real chaplains in my family: school chaplains, army chaplains, prison chaplains and I wouldn't have been surprised if we'd produced a chaplain to the secret service – not that anyone would have known.

Esso was silent for an unusually long time before saying, "Hang on! Didn't you tell us your old man died a couple of years ago – not long before we started here – and that it was an accident or something?"

I replied, "Yes. I told you he fell off the tower of our church – well, the one he was rector of – and the coroner's court gave an open verdict because they couldn't rule out suicide, but it was probably an accident."

"Yeah! Now I remember you said."

"For a computer-scientist, you've got a memory like a 1980's desktop pc."

"Yeah, but my processor's awesome. Anyway, what's changed to make them think it's murder. If it wasn't before?"

"At the time everyone said he'd been up there alone, as he often was, birdwatching. The women polishing the pews and the candlesticks said they'd have noticed anyone coming or going after he went up there. But now someone's come forward to say there were definitely two people on that tower at the time. He was hang-gliding and had a good view. So the police think whoever was there must have been responsible for my father's death or they'd have been there to explain what happened."

"But why's this hang-glider bloke waited years to tell anyone?"

"He says he didn't see the significance of what he saw. Didn't even know anyone had fallen off the tower. Then he read a piece in the paper about the new rector and it mentioned the previous one had died in that way. There was even a photo of the church, so he realised that was the one."

Esso said, "No wonder you're off your game. You sure you should be here? Don't you want time off to be with you family or anything?"

"It's funny. I think it's because we did all our crying and grieving back then. We've moved on. Or thought we had. Now, I don't know. I don't know what to think or feel. I mean, I always thought it didn't make sense. He went up there so often, he was always careful. Not that he'd have to try too hard to be safe. There was a sort of battlement thing round the top of the tower well up to your waist. He'd have to have tried hard to lean over far enough to fall over it. And as for suicide – forget it! He wasn't the type. He was so laid back, nothing got to him that badly and it was against his principles. He saw it as a serious sin, although he never said so to relatives of parishioners who'd killed themselves, obviously."

Esso cursed as we caught up with the Saturday afternoon traffic near the city centre. I refrained from telling him we should have taken the longer but quicker route via Western Avenue. He asked, "Do you know if they've got a suspect or anything?"

"If so, nobody's told me. I certainly can't think why anyone would want to kill him. Come to that, I can't think how anyone could've got up there without being noticed."

"Yeah. Right. They'd have to get out again without being noticed an'all." As a cyclist pulled out to pass a parked car without looking, he cursed again before asking, "Did you say you only heard about the murder the other day? Well, how come you've been, err, not your usual cheery self for weeks? What else is up?"

"I've not been happy doing theology and I'm wondering about giving it up, if only I could think what to do instead."

"Does that mean you don't want to be a vicar any more?"

"Yes."

"I can hardly see you as anything else."

I said, "That's what everyone says, but I've always had misgivings. I don't like dressing up and doing all the rituals and stuff. I tried to tell Father not long before his death, but he said it just meant I'd be what they call *low-church*, like my Uncle Andrew. He said I could sort out all my questions at uni or afterwards, at theological college. I think it was his death that made me go ahead and apply to read theology. You know, so as not to disappoint him."

Esso asked, "Your studies haven't helped, then?"

"No. They've made things worse. You see, until I came to uni, I hadn't worried about the basics of the faith. I'd just gone along with what I was taught in Church, in Sunday school and school as well as at home."

"Didn't you do religious studies at A Level?"

"Yes. But you know the public school I went to had a strong Christian tradition. Faith was hardly a problem. Once I started my studies here, I was amazed that most academic theologians don't believe the Bible at all. It was written centuries after the things it records and there are lots of bits that must've been altered or added later too and the writers must've put their own ideas about God into what they wrote. And it's all a bit dated by now, obviously."

The traffic had stopped. We waited. After what seemed like hours, we began to move. Esso sighed, "I thought we were gonna be stuck here for ages."

Then everything stopped again. A student we knew was strolling towards us along the pavement. I opened my window and called out, "What's going on?"

"Road works."

Esso leaned across and said, "Hang on! I didn't see a 'road works' sign and anyway, it's a Saturday. You don't mean council workmen work weekends now do you?"

"Must be an emergency. Could be a gas leak."

The cars in front of us began moving again and we followed without taking our leave of our source of information. When we finally got to the roadworks, water was covering the road and most of the pavement. Esso said, "Gas leak? Didn't the dozy dipstick notice all this water?"

"Calm down! It doesn't matter what it is. We're stuck in this for as long as it takes."

Esso said, "Speaking of things that don't matter, why are you so bothered about all the arguments about the Bible? Does it matter?"

"All the Church's teachings are based upon the Bible – well, sort of. I don't see how anyone can go on and be a vicar if they don't believe half the stuff they're spouting. I wish I could go and talk to Father. He must have sorted it out in his own mind. He can't have been a hypocrite, surely? He always seemed so assured of his faith. That's why I always believed everything he said about it."

"What about the other theology students? How do they deal with it?"

"Obviously, not all want to be vicars or anything. Some want academic careers, others want to go into something else but want to do a subject they enjoy for now. The ones who want to be vicars don't seem to have any problem with the issue. Some say it's OK not believing all that's in the Bible, so long as you do the job well. Others say it's a way of being a sort of social worker or political activist without having to fit in with the powers that be. I think there's a couple of those in my family, actually."

Esso said, "So you think the God-squad are right?"

"What?" I knew the God-squad was a nickname for the Christian Union. They tended to be evangelical non-conformists.

He said, "They say all you theology students are in it for the wrong reasons and lack real faith. They always surprise me at their simple faith, when you think that they're students, I suppose they must apply serious thought to the subjects they study, but not to religion."

"I see what you mean. Well, yes, they may have a point about theology students, but I couldn't be as unquestioning as them – about anything. Nor could you."

"I couldn't. Hmm. You are in a mess, aren't you? I'm afraid I can't help. You know me: not quite an atheist, but not exactly devout. I want to go into the IT business and make lots of money, just like my father."

"Is he in the IT business?"

"No way! He's just good at making money. I don't suppose I could tempt you – oops! Perhaps an unfortunate choice of words, but please think about it. If money doesn't make you happy, it lets you suffer in comfort. Oh! And another thing. Women like men with money, even the supposedly independent, selfreliant ones. Trust me. I know."

"I have noticed that you are never short of female company. I put it down to your good looks and charm. Do you think your family's wealth and your good prospects have something to do with it?"

Esso laughed, "I'm sure of it. Of course, it's nice having a dad and a step-dad who are both loaded. My real dad's a typical entrepreneur. He's managed to make money in several businesses. He's even helped my step-dad to do better."

"But he's a racehorse trainer, isn't he? Does your first dad know anything about horseracing?"

"No. He knows about money, and a racing-stable's a business – among other things. He says my step-dad had been too focused on all the rest of it until he had a chat with him about making it pay."

"So now I know the secret of your attractiveness to women."

"It all helps! By the way, a few women I know say they find you attractive, so don't think they all go for big strapping types like me. Some like little guys, especially tough little scrum-halves. But I don't think potential vicars are top of their lists."

I said, "Do both your father and step-father send you a lot of money? You never seem to be short."

He chuckled. "You know I do a bit of work for a company that investigates cybercrime for business clients? It pays well. So well that I've never had a student loan. I borrowed a bit from my father's business at first, but I've nearly paid it off now."

As we pulled up outside our flat on Cathedral Road, he asked, "What are you doing tonight?"

I checked my phone for messages as he unlocked the front door. "I suppose I'll do a bit of reading. I'll see what's on TV and I might make a few notes for my next essay."

"I think you need to go out and enjoy yourself. If you stay in you'll just get depressed."

"I don't feel like being the life and soul of the party."

Esso said, "You're letting things get on top of you. Tonight. I'm going to that dance in the students' union. I'm helping with the sound but I hope to find time for a few dances too."

I said, "And to fix yourself up with a woman for night. But I'm not in the mood."

"You will be once you've got a few beers inside you."

Chapter 2

In the end, I went with Esso to the dance, but I didn't feel like dancing. I sat with a beer watching the others. Some of their moves were impressive. Not always in a good way.

A small blond girl came and sat beside me. I nodded and grunted a greeting. She was quite pretty. I expected a lot of lads would have envied me, but I wasn't looking for a woman. I recognised her only when she spoke. "Hi Matty. You don't look like your usual happy cheerful self. What's up?" It was my sister, Janice. Questions flooded my mind, including why had I not recognised her at first.

"Shouldn't you be away at school?"

"You must work on your chat-up lines. That would get you off to a bad start."

"I'm not chatting you up. You shouldn't be here. Does Mum know?"

"God! You can be so boring. Almost like a grown-up."

"I am a grown-up – but you're not. You're not even a teenager!"

"Say that again! Not everyone heard you." She dropped her voice as there was a pause in the music while someone made an announcement. "I'm sick of being treated like a child. Anyway, don't you remember it was my thirteenth birthday only last month. You sent me card. Quite a funny one, actually. Thanks,"

The Key to a Murder *by John Harvey Murray*

"All right! I'm sorry if I seemed to treat you like a child. I know how annoying people can be when they assume you're younger than you are. It comes with being small. Never mind that - you haven't answered any of my questions."

She sighed. "All right. If it'll make you happy. It's half-term at my school and I told Mum I'm spending it with Uncle Francis and Auntie Barbara at Llandaff, which I am, but I'm going out tonight with my friend Zoe from school – who is here, by the way – and I told Auntie Barbara if it got too late I'd go home with her for the night. Her parents live just a stone's throw from here."

I thought it was only a long stone's throw to Llandaff, but before I could say anything, Jan nudged me and said, "Oh! There she is: dancing with that big guy."

I saw a girl dancing with Esso, who had apparently left the music to take care of itself. She was a redhead. She looked older than Janice, but I wondered how old she was. Worrying thoughts crossed my mind.

"How did you get in without a student's union card?"

"I used this." She showed me a card with a photo of someone who looked a lot like her.

Elizabeth Lloyd-Williams, University College, London.

I asked, "Did you pick her pocket?"

Jan gave me a pitying look. "She used to go to our school. Her sister still does. She's friends with me and Zoe. She lent us the card since she's away somewhere this weekend."

I realised why I hadn't recognised her at first. "The photo looks more like you than you do. Last time I saw you, you had straight hair like this Elizabeth whatshername-something, but now you've got it in ringlets."

"They're extensions! They make me look older. Look – stop quizzing me and tell me what's up with you."

"I'm upset because I've heard our father's death wasn't an accident – he was murdered."

"I know! Mum told me when I phoned the other day. She's in a hell of a state. I asked if she wanted me to go home but she says she's got half the ladies in the church buzzing around her. I'd only be in the way. I expect the same would apply to you." Our mother had said something similar to me too.

"So why are you so cheerful?"

"I did all my crying when I first heard he was dead. Of course, I hope they catch whoever did it, but I just don't feel the way I did. I mean, however you look at it, he's just as dead whatever happened."

I said, "Speaking of cheerful things - are you going to Grandad's funeral on Friday?"

"I suppose so. Mum says I'll be allowed time off school and she says we should both go because he was always fond of us. I was fond of him too, but I hadn't seen him for ages. Not since we used to go for holidays on the farm when we were kids."

I was glad to know we were no longer kids. For a moment I recalled our happy times on the farm. I had said

I wanted to be a farmer when I grew up, but my parents had steered me in another direction.

I said, "It'll be a help to Mum. You know she didn't get on with her brother and his wife. Neither did Grandad, come to that. Last I heard, they were living in Newport and he was working in a bank or something."

She prodded me, "Come on! It's no use wasting the evening. Let's have a dance."

I got up and let her lead me onto the dancefloor. I thought I was doing it just to please Janice and to save her from predators but I found myself enjoying it. When we paused for a breather, I said, "I'm going to get another drink but I don't want to get you one. It's illegal."

"You really have grown up, haven't you? Well, I don't drink alcohol anyway. Just get me a fizzy water."

When we returned to our seats, Esso and Zoe joined us. She said, "Oh, Jan, you've done all right. Nice one!" I was taken aback when I realised she was referring to me.

I leaned as close as I could to Esso and said, "This is my thirteen-year-old sister and that's her schoolfriend. Be careful." He looked at me quizzically. I nodded. He stared at Zoe.

She asked, "What's up? What's he said?"

He shrugged. "Nothing. I was just wondering, err… you know…"

Jan shook her head. "Listen, Zoe – Matt thinks you must be the same age as me."

Zoe giggled. "Don't worry, lads. We're not in the same class. I'm sixteen." She certainly looked old enough to be sixteen, not just because she was tall, but I noticed she glanced to one side as she said this. When the music began again, Esso and Zoe began dancing again. They seemed to be paired for the evening.

After a few dances, Esso returned to me, saying, "I've got to get back to work." He pointed to the console where he controlled everything. "Keep an eye on Zoe. I'll be back for her later."

We enjoyed the rest of the evening until Zoe said, "Listen, Jan, Esso's asked me to spend the night at his flat so we won't be going back to mine."

I said, "OK, Jan, I'd better walk you to Llandaff."

"Oh, no! Uncle Walter and Aunt Maggie and their little horrors are staying with them this weekend. Spare me that!" I felt sympathy as I too would have tried hard to minimise the time I had to spend with our Uncle Walter, Aunt Margaret and their brood.

Esso said, "We could all go to our flat for the night. We've got separate rooms."

I agreed, not quite as enthusiastically as Jan, who phoned Uncle Francis to update him on her plans.

Esso had a double bed, whilst there were two singles in my room. I cleared some debris from one and made it up for Jan. The dividing wall was not very thick and noises coming through left little doubt as to what Esso and Zoe were doing. Jan couldn't stop giggling for a long time. When she did, she said, "You know the new rector's about to move in? That's why Mum's moving out. Well, he says Bessie can stay for now but not for long. Where can we keep her? The new house Mum's getting doesn't have a stable or a paddock like the rectory. She says she couldn't afford anywhere with much land. I think she thinks we'll want her to sell Bessie because we hardly ever ride her, but I want to keep her. I always ride her in the school holidays."

"Now that really is bad news. I was thinking of getting a cart so we could drive her when we're home. And when I've finished my studies I might be able to live somewhere with a bit of land. Anyway, I'll be going home next weekend. Mum can't keep putting me off forever. I'll see what I can do." Bess was a Shetland pony who had been mine before I outgrew her and passed her to Jan. In our day, we had competed in Shetland racing, quite successfully.

As I was dropping off to sleep, Jan said, "I know who could've killed Dad."

"I thought you weren't bothered?"

"I didn't say that. Anyway, you've got me thinking."

I refrained from making the obvious quip and said, "Go on, then - tell me - who?"

"One or other of the women who were cleaning and tidying the church."

"Ridiculous!"

"That's what everyone probably thought, including me until now. But when you think about it, I'll bet any of them could've slipped away up the tower and not been noticed. And Dad would've been off his guard – not that he was ever on it – to see someone he knew well.

It wouldn't have occurred to him they might have had anything against him."

"That's because none of them had. I mean, what could he have done to make any of them hate him so much?"

"I don't know, but nobody's been looking into that. What if one of them's a psycho? Or if he stood between them and a load of money? Or say he knew something they didn't want anyone to know? He might not have known how desperate they were to hide it."

"I think you're letting your imagination run away with you."

I managed to get to sleep at last, but the thought Jan had planted in my mind kept coming back to me. I wondered if the police were checking backgrounds for motives? How to find out?

In the morning, Jan and I went to a service at Llandaff Cathedral, where our uncle, Canon Francis Chaplain, was one of the priests and lived in a house in its precincts. After the service, Aunt Barbara invited me to join them for Sunday lunch. I accepted, although I wished I had picked a day when her sister, Margaret, her husband Walter and their children were not present.

As we walked from the Cathedral to his house, Uncle Francis asked me how my studies were going. I replied, "OK academically, in that I did well in my last end-of-term exams, but I'm not happy, to be honest. I'm questioning my vocation."

"Perhaps you'd like to chat about it, before lunch, as I've been through the process, albeit some years ago.

It's all right, Jan, you don't have to put up with this. When we get home, Matt and I can go into my study and you can do whatever you want."

"Oh? Can't I join you? I've got to think about my future and nowadays girls can be priests too, you know."

We agreed to let her join us. I told them all that was bothering me. He listened sympathetically before saying, "I think you're worrying too much. To some extent, I think you've picked the wrong place to study. I went to a theological college in Oxford with a high-church reputation, so I got the kind of training I wanted. If you're low-church, there are some good places you could pick. Some universities are full of liberals with no idea about faith."

"Doesn't it bother you that the Bible might not be true?"

"Personally, I think a lot more of it can be substantiated than some people are willing to accept. But anyway, it depends what you mean by true. You know that Jesus taught by using parables." I nodded. He went on, "Well, those stories all made a valid point without being accounts of real events. What if other parts of the Bible were like that? If you get the message, it might not matter too much about the historicity. Perhaps that was what God intended."

"That's what some of my lecturers say, although you made it sound more reasonable."

"Apart from that, how are you coping with the rest of your studies?"

"I'm good at Greek but I find Hebrew a struggle."

Janice burst into the conversation. "Why do you need to study Hebrew anyway? Or Greek for that matter?"

I replied, "It's important to understand what the Bible actually says, and meant, rather than relying on what someone says it says. It's the same reason we do the history of the Old and New Testaments: to see what they meant at the time."

Uncle Francis said, "Good! What about the other elements of your course?"

"There's sociology and psychology of religion. That seems to be all about proving all religion is a human invention."

My uncle said, "So what? It shouldn't surprise anyone that God made our psychological and sociological natures so that we wanted and needed religion."

"Hmm. You've got a point there. Oh, and there's philosophy of religion. That seems to be a way of proving God can't exist. Mind you, to hear some of the stuff, you'd find it hard to believe we exist."

We all laughed. Then Uncle Francis asked, "Are these intellectual problems so serious that you want to give up the course? Or is there more to it?"

I hesitated before replying, "I've met lots of people who are going into the church for all the wrong reasons."

"What matters is *your* reasons. I don't give tuppence for what anyone else's reasons are. I know my own. Besides, it's amazing how God moulds people after they've gone into the priesthood. The effectiveness of the Church's ministry of the word and the sacraments doesn't depend on the worthiness of the clergy – thank God! None of us is really worthy, but God uses us in His own way."

Janice said, "I'll bet Matt will make a good priest. He's clever and also kind." She looked at me and added, "They say suffering strengthens you and makes you a better person. I think God's letting you go through a hard time so as to prepare you for His service."

My uncle said, "Speaking of suffering, how are you both coping with the latest bit of news about my brother's death being murder?"

Jan said, "It makes no difference as I've got over the shock of losing him."

He said, "I doubt that. Things like that often hit people when they think they've got over them. I know I'm still grieving. What about you, Matt?"

"The truth is that it comes and goes, not just from day to day, but sometimes from one minute to the next."

"Yes. That's how it is for me and for many people I've had to deal with in similar circumstances. It usually passes with time, but feel free to come and talk any time you want – either of you."

When he got up, I thought we had finished, but he said, "Let us pray." He then prayed aloud that God would guide me through my doubts and trials and into His will for me. I was amazed that he would pray in everyday language and with none of the props he usually used like regalia or incense. I was touched by the way he wanted to help but I remained uncertain as to my calling.

Chapter 3

During the week, I thought about my uncle's words but I still felt unhappy. Looking back, I think I had been blaming God for my father's death, ever since it happened. The news that it was a murder made it seem worse. Of course, you can't make a rational deduction that there is no god from any particular event, no matter how unfortunate, but coupling the emotional side of that with what I had learnt – or unlearnt – during my studies may have influenced my thinking.

I went to see the head of the management studies department. Since I had done well in my exams up to then, he was quite willing to give me a place on the course but I would have to start at the beginning of the three-year course at the start of the next academic year. He advised me to finish my theology degree, or at least finish my second year, and also to look into the question of finance. How would I pay my course fees and living expenses? Could I afford to take on another student loan? I was unsure.

On the Thursday, as soon as lectures were over, I went home to Amesbury near Salisbury. The familiar prettiness of the village was wasted on me. As I had feared, the news that my father had been murdered, arriving so soon after Grandfather's more natural death, had set my mother back. It was as if she was starting to grieve all over again.

The Key to a Murder *by John Harvey Murray*

On Friday, we went to Grandfather's funeral. It was held in the parish church in the village near the farm. The service was traditional, as he would have wanted. The vicar told a few stories about the deceased that were both amusing and insightful.

There was a reception in a hostelry not far from the church where Grandfather had been well-known. It was old and had been modernised, as well as extended, at various times, thus displaying several architectural styles. Likewise, the internal décor showed no sign of an overall theme. I thought the inconsistencies gave the place a character far more genuine and unpretentious than had it been carefully planned. I could image Grandfather being at home there.

Some of his drinking companions were there as well as family, neighbouring farmers and employees. I endured as much pretentious, self-centred talk from my uncle and aunt as I could before circulating among the people who had actually been closer to the old man for many years.

One of the most interesting was Gareth Morgan, who had worked for Grandfather most of his long life and remembered me with affection. I had not recognised him at first, as I had never before seen him in a suit. He said, "They don't read wills at funerals like they used to. I wouldn't mind knowing who's gonna get the farm. Your granfer said he wasn't leaving it to that son of his, on account that he's never shown any interest in it. Nor in his father, as far as I could see." He drained his glass and I got us each another cider.

The Key to a Murder *by John Harvey Murray*

Gareth continued, "He di say, once or twice as you and your little sister was the only relatives he had as had got the least bit of farming in you. I could see it. I remember how you loved having a go at everything when you visited. You loved all the animals too."

"I'm beginning to remember those days too. You know, the only thing I didn't like was the shooting. Grandad was always going into the woods, shooting things. I didn't like the loud bangs and I didn't like seeing dead animals and birds, even when he'd told me why they had to be shot."

"I expect you have to be brought up with it. Me and yer granfer used to go shooting a lot. Mind you, we were never as trigger-happy as some." He glanced around and smiled. "See that long lanky bloke? That's Jimmy James as farms beyond yer granfer's place. He can't get enough shooting. Comes onto ours when he's shot damn near everything in his own woods. We gotta look out, 'cos he's none too careful what or where he shoots and he's not even a good shot." He chuckled quite loudly.

After talking with some more strangers, I came upon a couple of about my own age. The man said, "I'm Owain and this is Mair. We work on the farm. She won't remember you, but I do. Back when we were kids, your grandfather used to have a horse that did a bit of work on the farm. You used to love sitting on the horse or riding on the cart. Me, I used to like playing on tractors or machines. I still do. That's my job now. You know, ploughing, reaping, all that stuff. Mair looks after the chickens and ducks.

The Key to a Murder *by John Harvey Murray*

On Saturday morning, several women from the church came to the vicarage to comfort Mother. They were well-intentioned, but I was unsure how helpful they really were. One had strong views on how to grieve, apparently unaware that people are not all the same. Another kept saying how awful it was and speculating as to what sort of person could possibly have done such a terrible thing. Some of them gave the impression they disapproved of my more rational, stoical response.

After lunch, I went to the church and climbed the stairs to the tower. I had forgotten what a long climb it was. I wondered whether spiral staircases were more tiring than the other kind. My fitness training for rugby did not seem to have been much help. I supposed I was using different muscles.

At the top I studied what was now a crime scene. Apparently the police had seen all they wanted to see and discovered nothing of any value regarding the investigation. Obviously, nothing had changed since their previous inspection when my father had apparently fallen accidentally. I didn't know what I hoped to find. I hadn't seen anything suspicious when I had previously been there. The marks on the stone parapet had weathered a bit. The initial opinion of the police had been that Father had struck the stones with his tripod. I supposed they could have been made in a struggle. Or not. I could see nothing the police had possibly missed.

I looked out at the familiar countryside. It was as pretty and innocuous as ever. The sun disappeared behind a cloud and the wind freshened. I began to feel an irrational fear. Was I going to fall to my death? Was some serial killer going to come out from a hiding place and attack me? There was no hiding place up there apart from the little turret covering the top of the staircase and there had been no one there when I came up.

The sky darkened. The wind became noisier. That wasn't the wind! Someone was coming up the staircase. They were almost at the top. There was a scraping sound of metal on stone. It occurred to me that there was no escape. The only way down was that staircase. Well, not the only, obviously.

I stared at the open doorway of the turret. It was so dark I could see nothing.

"How long are you going to be? Only I want to lock up in a minute. Haven't you seen all you want?" Mrs Wilson, the verger, emerged, waving a big bunch of keys.

"OK. Fair enough. Is that the time? I'll come now." As I went back down the staircase, I marvelled at this fiftysomething's ability to ascend it without seeming breathless.

My efforts throughout the weekend at finding a new home for Bess were unsuccessful.

****

When I returned to Cardiff, I told Esso about my weekend. He said, "I think you need to so something more cheerful next weekend. As it happens, I'm going to the races. My step-dad's got a few runners at Chepstow. You enjoyed it last time. Why not come along again?" It took me most of the week to decide. Well, no. I decided right away, then changed my mind. This went on lots of times until Thursday, when I made my mind up properly that something to take my mind off the mystery of my father's death and off the question of my calling would be a good thing. Esso said, "Great. I've already told them to expect you. I was pretty sure you'd see sense in the end." I wished I could ever be so sure about anything. He added, "Oh, yes. My real dad's going to be there with his latest wife and my new stepsister."

"Won't your stepdad mind?"

"Oh, no! My dad and my stepdad get on ever so well. I don't know my stepmum very well as dad married her only a couple of months ago and I'm not sure how long they were an item before that. My real mum won't care. She knows what he's like and says his other women – and there've been quite a few – are welcome to him."

On Friday afternoon at Chepstow, Esso and I went into the private box rented by a syndicate which included his father and stepfather among others. His mother, Vicky Fox, was a tall, well-preserved, redhead in her fifties. She was dressed to impress, with a big hat, a low-cut dress, lots of gaudy jewellery and all in bright colours. Some of my mother's friends might have described her as 'mutton dressed as lamb' but none of them could have carried it off with such aplomb.

Esso's father, Brian Peter Hoyle, was a big, well-built man with a dark complexion and long, dark hair that seemed to have a life of its own. He had a cheerful, jovial manner and welcomed me warmly, saying, "Glad to meet my son's flatmate and best friend. Sorry to 'ear about your old man. Dunno if anything I say can do any good. I suppose you've just got to keep going. That's life. Obviously, I 'ope they get whoever did it. For today, just try to enjoy the racing. I won't give you any tips, though. Let's wait for old Foxy to fill us in. He knows his horses and usually has a pretty good idea about most of the other runners."

He indicated the older of the two women with him. She was dressed in tweeds and oozed confidence. He said, "This my missus, Olive Smith. She refuses to change her name because she says there's no way she's going to be Olive Hoyle. So her daughter, Isobel – Izzy – still calls herself Izzy Smith."

Brian lit a cigarette and turned to someone else as Olive said, "Smith sounds somewhat common but there are some Smiths in high places, you know. Did you say your name was Chaplain? Oh! How interesting." She made 'oh ' into a three-syllable word. "I know a Chaplain who's a bishop in the House of Lords. A charming man and quite influential. Would you be related by any chance?"

I replied, "I'm not sure, but I've got relatives in lots of positions in the Church."

"I suggest you take advantage of whatever connection you've got with that one if you can. What's the point having connections if one doesn't use them?"

I thought her accent was upper-class but not quite genuine, as if she was trying too hard. Similarly, her

27

tweedy 'lady-of-the-manor' look seemed a little overdone.

She asked, "Do you go racing often?"

"Not really. It was good of Esso to invite me again. I used to ride in Shetland pony races when I was younger."

"I didn't know they raced ponies. One never hears about it." From her tone, I was not sure if she disbelieved me or disapproved of racing Shetlands.

I replied, "Perhaps it's confined to certain circles. There's quite a following in fact."

"Did you win much? I suppose you were an amateur if you were only young."

"Yes. I had a few wins. I won a few trophies. As you say, children don't get big money prizes. But I loved it for the thrill."

Olive turned to talk to someone else. Izzy came to me. She was small with short blond hair and wore a navy trouser-suit. She said, "So you're Charlie Chaplain! You're not quite such a shrimp as I imagined from what Esso said. Oh, it's all right - I quite like small men. Perhaps it's because I'm not so big myself. Are you doing computer stuff like Esso?"

"No, I'm doing theology."

"You mean you wanna be a vicar?"

"I did. I'm not so sure now. What about you?"

"I'm doing management studies at Bath Uni. Mum wanted me to do summat like English or history, but I heard you get a better load of blokes doing management. All future bosses. That's where the money is, not teaching English and that. If you give up theology, you wanna think about doing management. That'll lead to loads of opportunities. Brian agrees and he's no fool - knows how to make money."

"Strangely enough, I've been thinking of doing management studies if I give up theology. But I need some advice about money. I might have to take out another student loan. I really could do without that."

"Yeah! Too true. You wanna talk to Brian. I'll bet he'll know a trick or two to help and he won't mind. He's a good bloke and you're a pal of Esso's after all." She took aout a cigarette and said, "Mind if I smoke? Well, it's not a real cig. I've been trying to give it up and this is one of them vapes. So far I dunno how much use it is, to be honest."

"I don't mind, so long as you don't blow smoke in my face. I've noticed that vapes make more smoke than actual cigarettes."

She had just lighted her smoke when she sighed and extinguished it, as the caterers brought in the buffet. I was eyeing up the choice of sandwiches, pies and salads, hoping someone would soon announce that we could start eating, when Major Fox came in. Esso had told me that he was a former champion jockey. He was only about as tall as myself but was more generously covered with flesh. However, I could imagine he would have been the right build for a jockey when he was younger and fitter.

He said, "Good to see old friends and not-so-old ones." He chuckled at his supposed wit. "Hope you all have a good time. I suppose you don't need me to tell you that your horse, Red Heat, is in the second race today. He isn't going to win. Good for a place, though. The favourite, Devil's Advocate, should romp home. Not worth a bet, though. Odds are so short they make me – and this fellow - look tall!" He indicated that 'this fellow' was me. "Oh, sorry! No offense, eh?" I smiled and shook my head, as Esso and his mother cringed. The major added, "Good to see you again anyway, Chaplain. Keep this up and we'll be inviting you to join our syndicate."

"Thanks, but I must warn you I've not got much money."

"Not yet, eh? You just need to back a few long-priced winners, not that I can spot any likely ones on today's card."

Mrs Fox asked, "What about Liz? She is riding today? In with a chance?"

"She's in the race after Red Heat. She's on an outsider, Silver Rock. They're both inexperienced, so anything could happen. Long odds, so worth a flutter, if you like. After that, another one from my stable's in with a good chance in the last. Forest Oak, a plain bay. Hasn't done well lately, so we've got good odds. I reckon he's on top form now and should give the rest a run for their money. I'm afraid the price'll go up if he starts winning too often. So make hay while the sun shines, I say!"

Brian asked, "What about the first? It's a one-mile hurdle, isn't it? Got a horse in that?"

"Almost forgot. There's Dark Sea. He's one from my stable too. Another plain bay. He's had some bad luck lately, but seems on form now. Should get placed, so worth a small each-way bet, I'd say, and there's just about time to before the start, if you're quick."

The major helped himself to a sandwich and added, "Can't stop now. Lots to do. I'll be back later after I've seen Silver Rock's owner: some pop star, Johnny Whyte. Don't know what to make of him, but he pays his training fees, so that's all right!"

He waved a hand in the direction of the next box as he left. We all rushed to the bookies to bet on Dark Sea before rushing back to the box where we could watch the race in comfort. The major was right. Dark Sea was among the leaders most of the way round until he lost ground by stumbling over the last hurdle. However, he made a lot of it up again and finished third, which was a relief for those of us who had placed 'each way' bets.

After that, we watched the big chestnut, Red Heat, run a good race of two and a half miles, leading most of the way, clearing all the jumps easily, but failing to produce the extra burst of speed he needed when the favourite challenged him in the final furlong. Thus he finished second as his trainer had expected. Most of us made money by backing him for a place. Before collecting our winnings, we went to the side of the parade ring to wish Liz Lloyd-Williams good luck. Even in her racing kit, she did look a bit like my sister and I wondered if she knew where her student's union card had been. As we endured the blustery weather, Major Fox gave her a leg up and a few words of advice before the stable lad let go of the reins. Her mount was a pale grey, almost white and was not only the most beautiful in sight but also the best behaved. I hoped he would turn out to be one of the fastest.

As we headed back to the box, Brian Hoyle lit a cigarette, which was not a vape, and said, "I've 'eard you wanna change courses but you're worried about the cost if you 'ave to take out another student loan."

"That's right. I might have to stick with theology whatever course I prefer."

"Well, 'ow about borrowing for some other purpose? There's loads of low-interest loans available for certain things and even grants if you know where to look."

"Yes, but I do actually want the loan to pay for my studies not for something else."

We started climbing the stairs at the edge of the stand as he said, "You know that and now I know it. The lenders don't 'ave to know."

"You mean you think I should lie?"

"Well, I wouldn't put it like that. I'd just say you gotta be careful what you say." He blew some smoke before taking another drag and saying, "Why not start a business, like my Sam, and borrow more money than you're gonna need for the business? You can form a limited company quite cheap, or buy one that's what they call 'dormant'. That's one that already exists but ain't active. Know what I mean?"

"Yes, I get it, but wouldn't that involve a certain amount of err... dishonesty, if not actual lying?"

He shrugged as we reached the top of the stairs and entered the syndicate's box. He looked at his cigarette as he said, "Well, it might. Think about it anyway."

The Key to a Murder *by John Harvey Murray*

We watched Liz Lloyd-Williams ride to a disappointing fifth place on the unknown Silver Rock. They might have been placed, that is come in the first three, if he had not stumbled on landing after one fence halfway around, losing at least a length by the time he recovered.

Izzy came to me again and asked, "Was Brian any help?"

"He tried, but I'm afraid his suggestion sounded a bit unethical."

She held her vape aside and shook her head as she said, "Strewth! You'll never get on in business – or anything else, probably – if you wanna be ethical. You really are cut out to be a vicar, aren't you?"

We were still finishing the buffet when it was time for the last race which was a little over two miles. Forest Oak never moved up with the leaders until after the last jump. Then he found some extra speed and won by a nose at a good price. We had all chanced at least some of our money on him and so the day ended on a good note.

I told Esso I had enjoyed the day and was grateful to his father for his advice, but I was unsure about going straight from being a potential vicar to a life of deceit. Esso said he could think of people who would say there was no difference.

Chapter 4

When I next went home to Amesbury for a weekend, I found it impossible to talk to Mother about my career, as she was still in a bad state and was getting anxious about moving house. I couldn't burden her with another worry, as she had been hoping I'd follow the family tradition.

A letter was waiting for me from my grandfather's solicitors. He had left the farm to me! Sadly, I realised I would have to sell it. I could certainly use the money.

On Sunday, after the morning service, I left Mother with a group of ladies from the church and went to see Rev Arnie Armstrong, the man who had been our curate at the time of Father's death. He still was, technically, but had been suspended, pending a police investigation into a complaint of sexual assault by a woman in the parish. Father had never believed the allegation, knowing the woman as well as knowing the curate. The church authorities had opted to wait for the outcome of the police enquiries before commencing their own. The police had taken over a year before announcing, to nobody's surprise, that they were taking no further action since there was nothing to corroborate the woman's story. The church had then begun an investigation, which seemed to be going nowhere.

Arnie would have been a good-looking man if he had had two arms, but he had lost one, a few years previously, as a result of a motor accident, shortly before his ordination. This had left him prone to depression and he had developed a drink habit which he had tried to break on several occasions with the help of Ruth, his incredibly patient and understanding wife. The allegation and the response by the church had done nothing to improve the situation. Although most of the congregation had disbelieved the woman's story, several members muttered that there was never smoke without fire and similar cliches. There were some amateur psychiatrists who believed that his loss of an arm had left him with a chip on his shoulder, without noting how unfortunate was that choice of words. This chip had apparently made him feel a loss of manhood for which he had to compensate by inflicting himself on women, however reluctant they might be. Did they know where one's manhood resided? Not in the arm!

Ruth, welcomed me with a smile, but her usual cheerfulness had deserted her. She was as smartly dressed as ever, in a pleated skirt and matching grey blouse, but her makeup seemed to have been applied with less than her usual care and her hair, although tidy, had lost its lustre. She sat with me and her husband as we caught up with each other's news, but she was uncharacteristically quiet. After we went over what we knew about my father's death and the latest developments, Arnie updated me on the progress of his case, such as it was, and on the feedback he got concerning the local gossip. We agreed that my father would have been a big help to him in several ways at such a time, had he lived. After that I told him of my doubts about a career in the church and my uncertainty as to an alternative.

He said, "Aye, well, when it comes to the academic side, I studied in my home toon of Edinburgh and then in London and got to hear a variety of views. There are plenty of theologians with more traditional opinions. I could lend you a few books that might help."

He took a few specimens from a bookshelf. His dexterity with his one hand never ceased to impress me. As I flipped open the biggest and glanced at the contents, he asked, "Noo, are you sure it's parish work you're called to? There's lots of other types of Christian ministry."

"Do you mean something like youth work or children's work?"

"Aye, perhaps. But there's also the academic side. For all that you've seen, believe me there are some theologians who are helpful to us clergy. That's fine if you love studying and always want to delve deeper. You've got to have the right personality for whatever it is."

When I had pondered that for a minute, he added, "Your father told me he had a brother who was an army chaplain."

"Yes. Uncle Francis. He's a canon at Llandaff Cathedral now. What about him?"

"Your father told me your uncle used to train with the men so he could keep up with them in everything except combat. He said it was the best way to get their respect so they'll open up to you when they need to. Perhaps you could do something like that."

"I don't think I'd be up to that."

"Och! You're good at rugby and you used to be a jockey, did you not?"

"It was only in Shetland racing."

"Aye, but I'll bet it was demanding. Well, I think you could be an army chaplain if you saw that as your calling."

"It's a thought. But what about the way the church has treated you? I know that some of the church officials and even fellow clergy have been most unsupportive. As soon as the police got involved, my father said he and our family were almost the only ones who didn't avoid you or avoid talking about the elephant in the room, anyway."

I asked Ruth, "How have you coped?"

She looked at her hands in her lap as she said, "It's been, you know, pretty bad for both of us. I don't know how Arnie kept being civil to some of them. I mean, err, it's no wonder he's drinking again."

I asked Arnie, "Are you saying you wouldn't advise me to go into the church as a career?"

He looked sad as he replied, "To be honest, I canna say right noo."

"My flatmate is doing computer studies. He wants to make lots of money. I'm tempted to join him, although not in computers. I might try management science."

Ruth forced a smile and flicked her hair back, as she said, "If you find a way of making loads of dosh, do tell us. I mean, Arnie's stipend is far from generous and I'm afraid that if, well, you know, if things go badly, he might need a new career too."

Arnie said, "I hope you find the right thing for you, whether it's serving God or making money. I've no idea what I'll do if I get the sack. I've been so sure of my calling for so long."

I said I hoped the authorities would move him to another parish as soon as his suspension was lifted, which I assumed it would be, as there was no evidence apart from the word of the complainant, whose acquaintance with truth was known to be at best fleeting.

I went back to Cardiff and found the books Arnie had lent me to be a lot of help. I was determined to get some return for all the work I had put in. I discovered that I could get a degree, but not with honours, if I did well enough in my second-year exams. That should ensure I got onto whatever course I chose next. My biggest problem was money.

It was almost Christmas when I phoned home to sort out the arrangements for the holidays.

"You can NOT be serious!" I blurted out into my phone, not really thinking my mother was joking.

"That was my reaction," she replied. "The police are sure it was Arnie who murdered your father, although I just can't believe it. I mean, he was such a help - well, him and Ruth, when it happened, as well as since, despite his silly suspension that's been going on far too long. I'm sure your father would have kicked a few backsides and got them to get it sorted out by now if he was alive."

"Why? I mean, why do they suspect Arnie?"

"Well, I'm afraid it was something I said. Silly me. They said if someone was up that tower with Father, and if everyone who'd been in the church at the time insisted nobody else had gone up there after he had gone up, the killer must have got in by that outside door. You know, the one that leads straight to the bottom of the stairs up the tower. I told them it was always locked. Father insisted on that after he found a gang of kids playing in there. Just think if one of them had fallen off the top. Oh! No!" She started to cry.

When she sounded composed, I asked, "You said you told the police the door to the tower was always locked. So what?"

"Well, that's just it. They asked who'd got keys to that door and I said there was one on each keyring with all the other keys to the different doors in the church. Then they asked who had them. I said Father, the churchwardens, the verger and we kept a spare set at home for emergencies. Of course the curate had to have one too."

"I know he had a set of keys but that doesn't prove anything, does it?"

"That's what I thought, but it seems they asked poor Arnie and he said he'd had to hand his to Father when he was suspended. Then they asked me if that was true and I couldn't remember. So they checked with all the people I just mentioned and found we were one set of keys short and nobody could confirm that Arnie had actually handed his set in. I mean, it was just like Father to not bother if he hadn't."

"OK. What if he hadn't?"

"The thing is, that he said he had. They couldn't find a set at his house and why would he lie about it?"

"Did he have an alibi?"

"Not really. He said he was at home because he's not allowed to visit the church while he's suspended."

"What did Ruth say?"

"Well, she says he was at home, but she wasn't there the whole time and the police reckon there was just enough time for him to have slipped out and killed Father and slipped back again before she got back and she mightn't have noticed. Of course, she says it's rubbish. She'd have noticed. I mean, he would hardly have been acting like his usual self if he'd just got back from murdering someone, would he?"

"Did they say why he would have wanted to kill Father?"

"They say he must have blamed him for his suspension, which is piffle! Your father tried to help him. Everyone knows that. Unfortunately, in some people's eyes, that makes it worse. You know, biting the hand that feeds you, as it were."

"Have they actually charged him?"

"Oh, yes! They've even set a date for his trial, early in January."

Christmas was a nightmare. I had to be polite to everyone who asked about my studies or commented on Father's murder. I was tired of hearing how nobody would have thought that nice young curate could have been a murderer. I watched some racing on TV and saw Silver Rock unseat a professional jockey. In another race, Red Heat came last out of eight.

Chapter 5

I had been back at my studies for only a couple of weeks when I took time off to attend Arnie's trial in Salisbury. It was a trial for me and for Mother too. She said she had searched again and again for the missing keys, in case Arnie had actually handed them into Father. She had checked several times with each of the other keyholders. None had a second bunch of keys.

At first, it looked as if the prosecution's case was very flimsy. They began calling the hang-glider pilot and establishing that the man he saw with Father could have been Arnie. When cross-questioned by Arnie's barrister, he admitted it could have been a lot of people and that he had failed to notice how many arms the person had.

The prosecution continued by going over the question of access to the tower and the mysterious absence of Arnie's set of keys. The prosecuting counsel sounded confident until the defence made the senior investigating police officer admit that saying Arnie *could have* done it was not the same as saying he *did* it, although all the others with keys had been in the church at the time and, in effect, were each other's alibis.

The next witness was Mrs Taylor, the lady who ran the newsagents in the road by the church. She said she had seen Arnie outside her shop on the morning of Father's death. She had not come forward at the time, as nobody was suspecting Arnie and she did not know his presence in the street was significant. She said he had been talking to a customer who was just about to enter the shop. She said the man had given Arnie some change for the bus.

The prosecution pointed out that regardless of his reason for being in that street, Arnie had obviously lied about being at home all day and never anywhere near the church.

Ruth was then called as a witness to say that her husband's suspension had had a stressful effect on him and that his drink problem had reasserted itself with a vengeance. The defence counsel objected to the raising of the sexual misconduct complaint, as it had not been proven and was immaterial. However, the judge agreed with the prosecution's claim that it was relevant to the accused's motive.

This assertion was confirmed by the next witness, a psychiatrist, who claimed that Arnie's misfortune in losing an arm, coupled with his being accused, rightly or wrongly, of sexual assault, could have embittered him to the point where he might have focussed his resentment on some father figure and then believed murdering him would be the answer. He said 'might' and 'could' a lot.

The prosecuting counsel wrapped his case up by stating that Arnie had lied about his keys and his whereabouts. Why? Perhaps he had lied when he had said he had been grateful to the deceased for trying to help him. What if he had been far from satisfied with the help he had believed he was entitled to?

The defence did not call any witnesses or put Arnie up for cross-examination. They relied on a closing speech trying to dent the prosecution's case.

Arnie was found guilty.

On our way home, Mother said, "I can hardly believe it. I always thought so much of Arnie, as your father did – well, and yourself."

When we got home, I went for a long walk. I tried to tell myself that Arnie was not guilty. That there must have been mistakes in the investigation, flaws in the prosecution's case. But I couldn't see any. Arnie had not given evidence because he had none to give and would have come unstuck under cross-examination. If he was guilty, he must have been lying all along. He had lied to Mother, to Ruth and to me, as well as to the police. All the time he had been so kind to Mother, he was playacting. I could possibly have forgiven him for murdering Father if he had confessed and explained his reasons. Perhaps. But now he seemed a total phoney. Yet he was one of the most sincere Christians I knew. Or thought I knew. Oh God!

I wanted to see Ruth but didn't know what to say. I couldn't face her if she was still trying to pretend her husband was innocent but I supposed she would be the last person to accept that he had actually done it.

I thought my financial problems were almost over when I received a letter from a firm of solicitors informing me that my grandfather had left his farm in Monmouthshire to me. They mentioned that the delay in writing was due to the necessity of obtaining probate, which in turn required a valuation and the settlement of tax and other liabilities. On reading the enclosed valuation, I was more than a little disappointed to see how low a figure had been given: less than I had hoped for setting up a business and paying for the rest of my education. However, I instructed a firm of rural estate agents to begin the process of turning a notional sum into money in the bank. Janice phoned to say she had been left a sum of money but was told she was too young to obtain it directly and would have to let it be managed by trustees until her eighteenth birthday. She was even more disappointed when she discovered that I was not to be one of the trustees – they were all people she didn't know, including the solicitors.

When I went back to Cardiff, I told the head of management studies that I definitely wanted to enrol for the course starting that Autumn. I wanted to serve Mammon. Then I told Esso everything and said I wanted some more financial advice. He said, "We're all going to the races again soon for two days. It's the last meeting of the season and there's always a party afterwards somewhere. I'm sure you would be welcome. You can spend Friday night with us. On Saturday, it'll depend who's hosting the party. I think it'll be the Brecons this time. They've got a place not far from Chepstow, on the English side of the border. I've been before. They throw good parties."

It was a Friday afternoon, when Esso took us to Chepstow racecourse for the two-day meeting. Mrs Fox was wearing a different outfit from last time: more outrageously eye-catching with its loud contrasting colours and a slit up the side of the skirt as well as a lower neckline. Olive, Esso's stepmother, was again in tweeds. She said, "Have you seen Johnny Whyte? He's joined our syndicate and he's brought someone called Zig-zag. I don't know if it's a man or a woman. Nowadays, one can never be sure, especially with these showbiz types."

Izzy sighed. "Mother, these days nobody cares about gender or sexuality except oldfashioned prudes, and you couldn't fool anyone you were one of those, not even in your most boring outfit."

As I eyed up the sandwiches, another lady made a grand entrance. "Dah-lings! So sorry not to pop in earlier, but we've been entertaining Johnny Whyte, because our Liz is riding his horse again today. But I just had to leave my Tommy to look after him so I could be with my dear friends here." She went around hugging and kissing everyone. Esso nudged me and muttered, "This is Caroline, Lady Brecon, Liz's mum."

He had only just finished telling me, when the lady came to us. She was about the same age as Vicky Fox and equally well-preserved. She wasn't as tall as her but had an even more impressive figure, which her black and white dress showed off to advantage. A tiny but artistic hat was perched on top of a fantastic arrangement of blond hair. Her jewelry was more subtle than Vicky's but just as eye-catching. She hugged Esso and said, "My dah-ling Sammy - and who is this handsome young man?" He introduced me. "Delighted! A theological student? How wonderful! You must convert that heathen daughter of ours sometime." With that, she gave me a peck on the cheek and turned to greet someone else.

Esso added, "Liz is actually Lady Brecon's stepdaughter. Caroline, Foxy's first wife, moved in on Lord Brecon when the previous Lady Brecon was killed in a hunting accident. Liz takes after her real mother in looks and – if you ask me - in character."

When she had hugged and greeted everyone, Lady Brecon turned to face the majority present and declared, as if addressing the entire racegoing community, "Tommy and I are throwing a party tomorrow night at the new house to celebrate the end of the jump-racing season. Dear Johnny Whyte and his friend Zig-Zag will be with us and you are all invited. It won't be formal. Just come as you are." I thought most of those present were dressed smartly enough for any occasion, but I was glad I had made the effort to look smart.

I told Brian Hoyle about my inheritance and said I was interested in his ideas for using the money and was feeling less scrupulous than before. He said, "If you want to come and spend the night at our place, I'm sure we'll find time to talk money at some stage before we come back here for the final day's racing. I suppose you'll be coming with us to the Brecons' party afterwards?"

"I'd love to if you're sure it's OK. I mean, I hardly know them – after all, I've only met you once before now."

He held his cigarette in front of me and patted me on the shoulder, saying, "Don't worry, mate! I'm sure you'll be as well behaved as any of us."

The Key to a Murder *by John Harvey Murray*

Major Fox came in and said he was pleased to see me again, before announcing, "Our horse, Red Heat, has been going well. I reckon he's got a good chance today and he's got good odds too." I guessed that was because he had performed poorly in previous outings. "My other chestnut, Space Station is running in the second tomorrow and could be in with a chance. Don't bother backing Forest Oak in the last. He's not on form. Pick one of the longer-priced ones, but not a rank outsider. But watch out for my other bay, Dark Sea. He's on top form and could win the third tomorrow."

When the buffet arrived, Vicky Fox commented that I impressed her with my appetite, considering I was small and slim. Brian Hoyle guessed, rightly, that I took enough exercise to burn off the calories.

The trainer wolfed a sandwich and said, "Afraid I've got to go. Other owners to see and I've got to give a few jockeys some last-minute instructions. Still, you'll have my nearest and dearest to keep you company."

Lady Brecon asked, "To whom do you refer? The Vixen? Or is your latest mistress going to join us? Whoever she is!"

His eyebrows leapt up as he replied with a gasp, "Whatever can you mean? You know there's only one woman for me – the one and only Mrs Fox."

"One and only? I can remember when you said that about me. You don't mean to say you're still faithful to this one?"

Vicky Fox gave her husband a peck on the cheek, before saying, "Don't worry, my dear, I know the Brecon

Beacon is just jealous – and who wouldn't be? Now go and saddle lots of winners!"

Esso muttered, "My mother calls Lady Brecon 'The Brecon Beacons' because of her tendency to show off her buxom figure and she calls mother 'The Vixen' because she's a redhaired Mrs Fox. You might be forgiven for mentioning 'kettle' and 'pot'."

Brian asked, "How's things with that farmer, Hugh Evans?"

Vicky said, "Don't spoil a good day's fun by bringing that up!"

Her husband turned back from the door and said, "Saw him the other day. He's still going on about diversifying, whilst his son wants nothing but to be a dairy farmer. He says the market's better now that we've left the EU. His father says that's nonsense. I'll have to go and see them again sometime to try to sort things out."

I had to wait until we had seen the major's first runner, Red Heat, leave the parade ring with his jockey and all our hopes and best wishes, before I could ask what that was about. Vicky Fox explained, "My husband keeps some of his horses at the Evans's farm when they're not racing. The jumpers in summer and the flat-race horses in winter. Of course, a lot go back to their owners, but a few don't, including Red Heat, the one owned by the syndicate."

As we went back to the buffet, she said, "We're worried that if the farmer or his son goes ahead with taking the business in one direction or the other, they might not want the horses. If we're worried, all the syndicate should be. I reckon the syndicate should buy the farm and make sure it's run the way we want. They know what I think but some aren't sure. I will try getting Lord Brecon on side. He's got a few hunters he keeps at the farm too."

Vicky Fox giggled as she finished refilling her plate. "I might even get the Brecon Beacon to persuade her husband. She and I think alike on so many subjects – apart from each other. As you probably noticed, she says I'm a tart and I say she is!" She nudged me playfully with an elbow, making me nearly drop my plate. "You can observe us both at the party and make your own mind up."

We watched the next race, where Dark Sea didn't make any mistakes: he just didn't go fast enough and came eighth.

After that, Lady Brecon swept out of the box to rejoin her husband and Johnny Whyte in good time to watch his horse run in the third. Silver Rock was among the leaders all the way round and put on a decent burst of speed after the final jump but not enough to beat the first and second favourites.

Lord Brecon phoned and invited us to join Johnny's celebrations in his box, despite the fact that there were still a few races to be run. Seeing his horse placed was a good enough excuse for Johnny, apparently. We went.

Johnny was as impressive a sight as any of the ladies. He wore a white suit, shirt and tie. His hair was almost white and was sculpted into a work of art. He was in such high spirits that it was hard to believe his horse had come only third. Lord Brecon stood with him. He was of average size and conservatively dressed, but his lively face indicated that he was no dullard. He gave everyone a glass of champagne and invited us to help ourselves to refills.

Liz had changed into jeans and a pullover. Her long blond hair was tied back with a ribbon. She was slim and not tall, but bigger than I had imagined a jockey would be. I was to learn that National Hunt jockeys were often larger than those who competed in flat races.

Johnny said, "I've had a great day and Liz obviously gets on fine with Silver. I want them to stay together. So I'm telling the major to give her the ride whenever Silver's racing."

The major shook his head. "I know she has done quite well today, but Lady Elizabeth is only an amateur and an inexperienced one at that. I would strongly advise you to let me select the jockey for each race. Not all courses are the same and we haven't yet determined which is Silver's best distance, nor the best strategy for winning on him."

Johnny said, "Are you having a laugh? That so-called professional made a right cockup of the job at Christmas. I mean, you told me he'd been holding the horse back to save him for the final challenge, but he overdid it. I could see Silver seemed to lose interest after a bit. He'd have done better to let the animal do what it wanted. At least Liz works with the horse, not against it."

The trainer began to protest, but Johnny went on, "All right – I'll let you sort out the races for him and advise Liz about how to ride each one, but I want her. But there's another thing. You don't get it, do you?"

We all stared at him as he gulped down a glass of champagne and refilled it.

"Listen! I'm in showbiz, right? Having a racehorse is part of my image. That's why I had to have a white one. And one with a nice nature. I've sat on him a few times for publicity shoots and stuff. Having a girl jockey - and a real looker - makes us a bit more interesting. Of course, I want Silver to win and I'm sure he will, sometimes. But it's OK if he doesn't, so long as he doesn't come a cropper or anything."

Liz managed to get a word in. "He won't do that. He's a good jumper. Remember that stumble we had the first time? As I told the major, it was my fault. I held him in a bit before the jump so he put in a short stride and went up steeply, which meant we came down steeply too. If I'd let him have his head, he'd have cleared it in a big leap. As it was, he sorted himself out and got us both out of trouble. He doesn't just look good. He's great and has a lovely temperament. He's just right for someone like Johnny."

Fox knew when he was beaten. "OK – fair enough – if you two are happy, so am I. If you're to ride as often as Mr Whyte wants, you'd better apply for a professional licence as soon as. It will mean abandoning your studies, I fear."

She shook her head. "I can do both. I might have to miss lectures sometimes, but not that often and I can study at other times to keep up."

Her father tried to refill his glass but gave up on realising the bottle was empty. He looked pensive as he said, "It seems to me that you're taking on too much, but it's your choice. Good luck if you think you can pull it off."

"Thanks! I'll choose between careers if and when it's obvious that I can't do both."

Johnny said, "That's my girl. Now, let's fix a date for a photo op. We could do it at the stables if nobody minds? Me, you and the horse – all right? Oh, and the trainer, of course!"

Everyone agreed.

Johnny finally introduced us to his companion, Zig-zag, who was an enigma, being apparently of mixed race and indeterminate gender or sexuality. Zig-zag said, "I'm as delighted as Johnny with Silver's performance – and Liz's. I hope I looked OK in the photo."

Johnny explained, "Yeah! Some geezer took one of us all just after the race: Siver, Liz, Zig-Zag and me – plus the major, of course. I ain't seen it yet, but I know we all looked happy."

He then turned to Liz and said, "OK – that's all the racing for you and Silver for this season, but don't disappear! I want you both to be around for a few more photo opportunities and stuff. And you're always welcome at my gigs and my parties. Just you – not Silver! There are limits."

I didn't bet on anything in the final race of the day, when Forest Oak did worse than predicted by falling at the second last fence, but neither he nor his jockey suffered any injury. Esso and his father made some money by backing horses that were placed, but it was Vicky Fox who picked the unexpected winner.

That evening, Esso and I dined out with his father, stepmother and step-sister at a restaurant in Bristol.

After the starter, Olive said, "Izzy! You've ordered a fish main course."

"Yeah. I know."

"But you've used your fish knife and fork for your starter." She tried to get the attention of a waiter.

Izzy said, "It's all right. These'll do."

"Nonsense! Let them fetch you the correct cutlery!"

Izzy sighed as her mother persisted until she succeeded in catching a waiter.

As she began to eat her main course, Izzy turned to me and said, "So you've seen the light, eh? Gonna give up religion and that and join the rest of us?"

"Well, I don't know, but I wouldn't be comfortable preaching stuff I didn't really believe."

"Yeah, right. At least you can believe in money. It's definitely real. The thing I like about racing is you can have a good time and make money – if you know how. Obviously, for a lot of punters it really is a mug's game. But us lot in the syndicate are no mugs." She smiled at Brian before concentrating on her food for a minute. Then she said, "Why don't you join our syndicate? It could be just what you need. When you've made a bit of money out of it, you'll be able to set yourself up in whatever business tickles your fancy."

"If I had any money, I might. Did you have enough to buy a share in it then?"

"Yeah. My old man – my first one, not Brian – left me a bit as well as Mum when he popped off."

"Was he a businessman too?"

Before she could reply, her mother said, "Oh, yes! He made plenty of money out of property. He used to buy houses and sell them just when the market moved. Oh, and he used to buy plots of land and hold them until they got planning permission and then sold them to builders. He was good at getting planning permission."

Izzy added, "Yeah, he had friends on one or two councils. Well, that's what you need, if you wanna succeed in that business. Know what I mean?"

I nodded. I knew exactly what she meant.

Chapter 6

In the morning I had a second chat with Brian about money as we walked together around his extensive garden. It was so well maintained that I was not surprised when I discovered they employed a professional gardener. He was busy digging something up and paused to greet us as we passed. I reminded Brian of my situation.

"What you need, is to start a business and borrow money to develop it. There's loads sloshing around for new startups. Then borrow more than you intend to spend – at least for now – and use the spare instead of a student loan, see? It's not stealing. You can pay it back once your business starts making a profit. Once you've got a bit of money in the bank, you can invest some of it in the syndicate if you're interested. That should bring in a good return pretty soon. What they call a fast buck."

"I've no idea what business to even think about."

"Why not agriculture? There's grants and loans for that. You won't even have to buy a farm. From then on you can let it run itself, employing the men who were working it before. Then you can get grants for improvements and stuff like tourism. if it does B and B."

"So I'd have to call off the sale of the farm?"

"Yeah – don't waste the opportunity that's landed in your lap. All you have to do is borrow money to improve it both as a farm and for tourism. You'll need a business plan, but you can borrow one I did and adapt it."

The Key to a Murder *by John Harvey Murray*

We stopped to look at a small pond and Brian said, "There are goldfish in there but I don't think we'll see any just now. The shrubs behind it shade it so the fish won't fry in hot weather and so birds won't see them too easily. They come to the surface at feeding time."

I stared and thought I saw something move in the water. I said, "Do you think I should use my home address for business or the flat I share with Esso?"

"Use the farm. Say you live there. You'll wanna go there a bit anyway so you can make the plans realistic and keep an eye on what's going on, but don't get too involved. Consider yourself an investor not a farmer. I'd say you're better off saying you live in Wales, so you should be acceptable to the Welsh authorities. They've got money for tourism and agriculture to spare. Every now and then you should ask for more money for more improvements. They'll love that. Shows you're not letting grass grow under your feet."

I refrained from saying that farmers were supposed to let grass grow. I said, "I like it, but I haven't got any money to start with and I've got a massive student loan to pay off."

"Startup businesses are all the rage. They get to be first in the queue. Don't worry! If you're stuck, I'll lend you a bit and I won't expect you to pay me anything until you can afford it. So long as the paperwork shows you've spent the money in the time allowed, you'll be fine. If the worst comes to the worst, you can pay me and I'll pay you back straight away. You'll need more than one bank account, of course. I've got quite a few."

The Key to a Murder *by John Harvey Murray*

When we went back into the house, he took me to his office and I sat looking at some of the documents he downloaded from various agencies. It looked daunting at first, but once I had studied everything for a while, I saw how I could meet all the requirements. On paper.

In the first race of the Saturday afternoon, which was another one-mile hurdle, Dark Sea came almost last due to getting off to a poor start and, despite making up a lot of ground during the race, he was still well behind the leaders when they reached the finish.

After that, we watched Space Station, win over a distance of two and three quarter miles. Although not the fastest horse in the race, he cleared all the jumps easily and was still going strong right to the end.

The next race was the most prestigious and remunerative of the day, in which Red Heat won by leading from the front and staying there, this time producing the necessary acceleration when challenged in the final furlong. Everyone in our box hugged everyone else. Some had made a lot of money. I had made enough to be pleased.

That evening there was the promised party. The new house looked pretty old to me, but lacked character. It was a four-storey cube of reddish bricks with windows at regular intervals in all the walls and a couple of steps leading up to the plain oak double doors at the front. Inside, however, things were more interesting. Furnishings and objects had apparently been collected from all over the world over several centuries. There were paintings of various kinds on most of the walls, including a lot of portraits. I would have loved to know the story behind each item, but this was not the moment to ask.

Over dinner, Zig-Zag said to Liz, "You've a good appetite for a jockey. I thought you lot lived on air."

Liz swallowed another chunk of steak before replying. "Didn't you hear? The jump-racing season finished today. So I'm not racing now until Autumn. Tonight I'm making the most of the opportunity to eat things I like. I'll start dieting again in a couple of months."

Lady Brecon said, "I wish I could control my weight as easily as you do. I'm constantly fighting to keep mine under control." With that, she helped herself to another helping of roast potatoes.

Vicky Fox said, "Your self-discipline is an example to us all – in so many ways." Lady Brecon appeared not to see the point of that remark, but several other diners, including Esso, nearly choked.

Throughout the evening, it was hard to tell whether the barbed exchanges between 'Vicky the vixen' and 'The Brecon Beacons' were serious or playful. Just after dinner, I noticed a framed photo of a freshly-crowned beauty queen who looked like a younger version of Lady Brecon. Vicky Fox saw me looking at it and said, looking pointedly at Lady Brecon, "It says Miss Wales on the sash, but I can't see the year. It's not this year as they haven't had the final. Was it last year or the one before?"

Most of the others found this amusing, especially Lord Brecon. His wife smirked and said, "I can't remember. Which year was it when you won?"

Esso whispered to me, "Mother did enter it once or twice, but never won."

Vicky Fox said, "Caroline! You're such a tease. Shall I tell them what you used to do for a living before you found a rich man?"

"I'll tell them. It's no secret. I was a model. I worked for an agency and did a lot of publicity work, sometimes in person, sometimes just being photographed."

Vicky added, "In a state of undress!"

"I'll show you some of my photos. They're sexy but not indecent. You're just jealous that you haven't got my looks."

She dug out a photo album and showed us a few more pictures saved on a computer. She was a very good-looking woman and made the most of her assets.

I kept meeting new people and struggled to remember their names and other facts about them. I was glad I knew a few people there as I enjoyed watching several young and not-so-young men trying to outdo each other to impress Liz and Izzy, who both seemed far more interested in Johnny than anyone. I tried to discern whether he was interested in either or just teasing Zig-zag, who laughed a lot but sometimes gave Liz or Izzy looks that I couldn't quite interpret.

At one stage, I found myself sitting next to Liz. I asked, "What do you do when you're not riding racehorses?"

"I'm reading Zoology at University College London."

The Key to a Murder *by John Harvey Murray*

"Hoping to learn how to breed winners?"

"No. I want to work for an environmental charity, protecting rare species."

"That sounds interesting. I suppose that would mean travel?"

"Possibly, but a lot of the research work is done in this country. And we need to look after our own wildlife better. What about you?"

"I'm doing theology in Cardiff."

Liz raised a single eyebrow. "Oh? Planning on becoming a professional godbotherer?"

"Mmm… I was, but I'm having second thoughts."

"Realised all that religion stuff's a sham? At least you twigged it before it's too late to do anything else."

"That's not quite it. It's a bit complicated. Of course, all the zoologists I ever met were atheists. So I'm not surprised that you're one."

She smiled lopsidedly. "Well, what do you expect? Do you really think your God created everything in the universe in just seven days?"

"Strangely enough, that's not what bothers me. My father believed the Bible but said seven days didn't have to mean seven times twenty-four hours, just seven stages. And the Bible doesn't say 'There's no such thing as evolution'. I could study zoology without it causing me any conflict of belief. The real point of the story is that God created the world. That seems obvious if your only religion – even if you reject it – is Christianity. But if you didn't have that background, you might think the physical world had already existed and God had merely added a spiritual layer to it. But we believe everything is God's."

"Ooh! You have been awake in lectures, haven't you? I still think it's hard for a scientist to take the creation story seriously."

"I think you lot get too hung up on the first chapter of the Bible and don't look at the rest of it. There's so much more to it than the creation story, important as it is."

"Yes – there are lots of so-called miracles for the gullible."

"How do you define a miracle? Something your science can't explain?"

"Something that couldn't possibly happen."

"That's not very scientific."

"What do you mean?"

"The scientific approach means observing events and producing theories that explain them: not rejecting those that don't fit into your existing view of the world. If you get new information, from any source, you're supposed to revise your theories, aren't you?"

"Perhaps we would if there was any evidence for any of these miracles."

"Isn't the Bible itself evidence? Aren't there lots of stories of miracles all down the ages too? Aren't you lot being selective in the 'facts' you're prepared to consider when you produce your theories?"

Another young man had overheard some of our conversation and sneered, "You religious nutters don't half talk a lot of bollocks."

I replied, "Is that a considered scientific opinion?"

"You Christians just believe what you want to believe."

"How do you know what I want to believe? Come to that, how do I know atheists don't reject God because they don't want to believe? What if they fear that if there is a God, they could be in trouble and so they try to comfort themselves by saying there isn't one."

"You're pathetic!"

Liz scowled, making her look remarkably fierce, as she said, "Do you want to know what I think is pathetic? Putting someone down when they say something you don't agree with, without coming up with any rational criticism. At least Matt's got the balls to stand up for what he believes even if it's unpopular."

The defender of atheism went to inflict himself on someone else. Liz said, "If you've not lost your faith, what's turning you off theology?"

"Several things. I won't bore you with my problems. Trouble is – what to do instead? I'm looking at ways of making money. I'll need to pay off my student loan whatever happens."

"Oh, God – no! Money's boring. Everyone thinks it must be great coming from a rich family, but there's more to life than that. That's why I want to do something worthwhile, like saving nature. But I also want to be a success at something, like being a jockey. See?"

"I see all right, but it's OK to be blasé about money when you've got plenty. Ordinary lads like me need to get the money sorted out before we can think about anything else."

"I suppose. But being a vicar or something would be different – more interesting than an entrepreneur or whatever, as long as you can believe all that Bible stuff."

I was beginning to find the conversation interesting when someone else buttonholed me and told me religion was all a con. He seemed to be even more under the influence of alcohol than I was and I knew arguing would be pointless. By the time I had got away from him, Liz had disappeared.

At breakfast, I sat near Liz and said, "This is an amazing place. Is it OK if I explore?"

She raised a single eyebrow again as she replied, "Mind you don't get lost. Perhaps I should show you around. Oh, God! I promised to show Johnny around too. I'm beginning to feel like a tour guide."

"Just me and Johnny? Sounds like an exclusive tour group."

"Well, Esso's not up yet. And Zig-zag and a few others have skipped breakfast and gone for a run."

"Where? In the grounds?"

She laughed. "This is a big house with some nice gardens, but it's not an estate. We've got one of those up in the Brecon Beacons – don't laugh! I know what Vicky Fox calls Mother. No – they're running around some of the lanes. They've taken Sooty the labrador with them. He'll guide them back home if they lose their bearings."

Johnny joined us and asked if the tour was still on. It was. Johnny asked a lot of questions, revealing a considerable knowledge of antiques and of art. His accent was more refined than that which came across in podcasts and media interviews, although not as exaggeratedly so as Olive Smith or as naturally upper-class as Vicky Fox or Lady Brecon, compared with whom Liz sounded like a normal person from the south of England.

I asked Liz, "How far back does your family go?"

She shrugged and replied, "Everyone's family goes back as far as everyone else's. I suppose *you'd* say as far as Adam and Eve. Otherwise, well, back before the Stone Age. It's just that some of us have better documentation than others. Not that I know anyone who can trace their family tree back to the Stone Age."

Johnny said, "These days you need it in case the Home Office gets onto you and tries to have you chucked out as an illegal. My family came here just before the War, from Germany. My great-grandfather didn't get on with Nazis."

Liz said, "As far as I know, there's been a Lloyd or a Williams among the higher ranks of society as far back as the Middle Ages, before Wales was taken over by the English. Obviously, my ancestors decided collaboration was more profitable than resistance, at least most of the time."

Johnny asked, "Why do you call this your new house? Not been here long?"

"Oh no! We've been here ages. It's just that we've owned crumbling ruins in Wales even longer. One of my ancestors had this place built in the eighteenth century with the money he'd made out of his shrewd investments."

I asked, "What in?"

"I don't know." She looked at me hesitantly before adding, "I expect there was some connection with the slave trade. It seems everyone who made piles of money had such connections. But we've never seen evidence he actually owned slaves, although I suppose that's not the point."

There was an awkward silence until Johnny waved a hand at a line of portraits and asked, "Do know who all these characters are?"

"I should, but I forget at times."

A voice came from across the room. "You really should! If it was not for them, where would you be?" An old lady was sitting in an armchair with her back to us.

Liz said, "Morning Grandma! This is Matthew and this is Johnny. It's all right for you. You knew half these people personally, didn't you?"

"Cheeky girl! I'm not as old as she thinks, boys. But I did know that handsome fellow." She pointed to a painting of a man in military dress uniform. Something about the painting suggested the twentieth century. "That was my father. And that one next to him with the moustache was my father-in-law, a previous Lord Brecon."

"Thanks Grandma. We'll leave you in peace now. Sorry to have disturbed you."

"I don't mind being disturbed by two handsome young men. Especially ones who are interested in the house and the family, unlike so many of today's philistines who are interested only in pop music and so-called celebrities. Any time you two chaps want the full story, do come again and ask."

When we left the room, Liz hurried us around a corner and said, "I'm glad you're not obsessed with pop music and celebrity culture, Johnny!"

We all laughed for a full minute, until Johnny said, "The old lady's got a point - that's why I do try to take an interest in lots of things. There are so many aspects of life that repay your interest if you open your mind."

"I agree. Matt and I were talking last night about his ambition to make lots of money instead of going into the Church. I say money's boring. What do you say?"

Johnny said, "Wow! A heavy conversation at a party? Whatever next? Me? I want more than money. Of course, I'm doing OK in that respect nowadays, but what I love is fame and success. I get such a buzz from the applause of the fans at my performances. I'd hate to just sell recordings. I get why you love racing. And I'm glad you love horses like I do. Not just the way a motor-racing driver loves his car, but as friends."

As we stopped to look at an abstract painting and speculated as to its intended meaning. Johnny said, "OK so I'm not exactly into religion, but I respect those who are and I think priests and whatnot sometimes do a lot of good. I know some do a lot of bad stuff too, but then, so some singers and everyone. Are you sure it's not for you? I'll bet it's a more interesting life than making money."

I said, "Speaking of horses, I love them too. Don't laugh, but I used to do Shetland racing when I was a kid."

Liz raised both eyebrows. "Laugh? Why? I think it's great. That's how I started."

"Thanks. A lot of lads at school teased me about it. So do some other people."

Johnny said, "Well more fool them! I'll bet it takes skill and guts to ride in a race on a Shetland or a thoroughbred."

I said, "To be fair, some of them might have thought like Esso, who said even a shrimp like me would be a bit much for a pony no bigger than a labrador."

Liz glanced at the ceiling, which was one of the few not to be decorated in an interesting way, before saying, "He must've seen miniature Shetlands and thought the ones we raced we no bigger than them."

Johnny said, "I've read that where they come from – the Shetland Isles, obviously - the people used to use them for everything on the farms and that. I dunno how big the islanders used to be, but the ponies must've coped all right. They must be a lot stronger than they look."

Liz said, "Like me – and Matt, I'll bet!" She gave me a playful push and I pretended to stagger away for a few yards.

I asked Liz, "Do you have any horses of your own? Not racehorses."

"That's a sore point. We keep a few cobs at one of our Welsh castles so we can ride in the mountains, but we've no grazing here. We keep a few horses at the farm where Foxy keeps the horses not in training, but the owner's trying to sell it. It's all about money and taxes and … Oh God! I'm getting boring."

"Strangely enough, I've just inherited a farm. Perhaps Foxy and your father should look at it. In fact, I want to go and see it soon. It was my grandfather's and I haven't been there for years."

"Why not? Talk to Daddy. He'll be busy all today, but there's always tomorrow."

"Will he see me?"

"Why not?"

Johnny said, "Here – hold on! That farm you mentioned's the place Silver's gonna be living innit?"

Liz replied, "I'm sure Foxy's got somewhere in mind if they have to leave that farm."

Johnny said, "That's what he keeps telling me. But it's always so vague. I need Silver where I can get him when I want for photo ops and stuff. And I want someone to ride him a bit so he won't get too fat when he's not racing. So it's no good if they find somewhere in the back of beyond."

Liz stretched. "Don't fret. Old Foxy's no fool. He'll see it's all OK. Mind you – it would be neat if your place was near enough and you'd let Daddy and me keep our horses there and Foxy could keep the ones he sends there. You wouldn't mind, would you?"

"I can't see why I'd mind. But I only want to treat it as an investment. You see I don't want to be a farmer."

Chapter 7

That afternoon, I phoned the farm and told Gareth Morgan, one of Grandfather's old employees, who remembered me, that I was bringing a few people to see the place. He was delighted that Grandad had left it to me, he thought I'd make a good farmer. Then Lord Brecon drove me, Liz and Johnny in his Range Rover to the farm that was about halfway between Chepstow and Monmouth. I had a look at the outside of the farmhouse and the other buildings. The house was almost derelict, but the outbuildings looked serviceable.

I said, "See those three terraced houses? I remember they used to be tied cottages but Grandfather has been letting them out to tourists."

Lord Brecon said, "You could live in one and let the others before you got the main house sorted out – which you certainly would need to do."

We looked across the fields and onto the surrounding hillsides, over which sheep were scattered. Liz asked, "Do you know how many sheep you've got?"

"No. I'll have to ask. I can see the Hereford cattle over there, but there used to be Holsteins on the other side for milk, but I don't see any."

We walked along a line of empty stables and around the end where there was a caravan before going to the farmhouse, where we were met by Gareth Morgan, who looked more himself, being in his working clothes.

He led us into the house and made a pot of tea in the kitchen.

I told him I was thinking of keeping the farm but only as an investment. He looked sceptical. I said I would need to employ someone to do the farmwork as I did not intend to do it myself. He said, "Well, I'm getting ready to retire. I'll hang on if you like, and see what you decide, but I'll be giving it up soon. Don't reckon I'll manage farming for another winter. The others'll manage I expect. There's a lad, Owain, who lives in the village. Him and his missus, Mair, do most of the work. Mair looks after a few ducks and hens but Owain likes driving a tractor. Then there's the herdsman, William Williams. You'll see him, I expect. He lives in one of the cottages there but he's got a job in the village now. Just keeps an eye on the cattle and moves them between fields at the right time."

I asked, "What about the sheep?"

"They're not ours. Since your granfer gave up his sheep, he's let his neighbour over there graze on them top fields."

"Didn't he used to have Holsteins as well as Herefords?"

"You remembered? He sold off the Holsteins a couple of years back when all the milking and that became too much for him – and for me."

Lord Brecon asked, "Do you have any horses here?"

"Not now. We did have a few liveries. There was a woman as looked after them. Lived in the caravan by the stables. She give up when a couple of owners moved their horses away and she took hers with her."

Lord Brecon said, "The stables look in good repair. If anyone wanted to keep horses here again, there'd be nothing to stop them?"

"As long as they got a groom. Could have the caravan or one of the cottages, I suppose."

Gareth looked past me. I followed his gaze. It seemed to be fixed on a gun-cabinet. He asked, "Do you shoot?"

"No. I never have."

"One thing your granfer and I always used to do was keep down the vermin."

"What vermin?"

"Crows mostly. Then there's rabbits and foxes. Since they banned hunting, them foxes have been getting cheekier all the time."

"What about rats and mice? Aren't they as big a pest as foxes and the rest?"

"They are. We get a man to come and see to 'em once in a while. Uses poison. I'll give you his number if you like."

"I don't intend to be here enough to shoot and keep the rest of the vermin down."

"Well, it won't matter. The neighbours on both sides love shooting and your granfer used to let 'em come onto his land when they liked. Just as me and him used to go over onto theirs at times, see? We told 'em when we were going. They usually tell us, but they do forget at times. Shall I tell 'em it'll be all right with you if they carry on?"

"I'd be grateful."

The others had been listening quietly but apparently interested. Now Liz said, "I think you'll need to keep a gun, Matt, just in case. Farmers always do, even absentee ones."

Johnny asked, "What sort of guns are you talking about?"

Gareth nodded. "Come and have a look."

He unlocked the cabinet and took out a gun. "Now this is an old-fashioned double-barrelled shotgun. There's a fancy new one. Pump action they call it. The old man did say I could have it. There's nothing in writing, but I'd like to keep it."

I said, "Please, keep it. That's fine."

"Thanks. Now, see how this old'un works. You break it like this to load or unload." He pressed it down onto his knee and it opened, revealing the rear end of the two barrels. "You can see where the cartridges go in, right?"

"Yes."

"Mind you keep it broken like this whenever it's loaded. That way, even if you bump into summat or drop it, it won't go off. Only carry it unbroken when it's not loaded, all right? Don't be like the bloody fool I used to know as shot hisself climbing a stile with a loaded gun in his hand."

"I will certainly bear this advice in mind if I do decide to do any shooting. Thanks."

"Remember you gotta keep it in the cabinet and keep it locked, whenever you're not using it. It's a bit of a nuisance, but it's the law nowadays and I suppose it stops people having more accidents. Oh, and you'll need a licence. Shouldn't be no trouble, 'less you got a criminal record." He chuckled at the thought. "Don't worry. If you say you're a farmer they'll give you one as soon as look at you. They know farmers don't go around playing cowboys and Indians." He chuckled even louder. Lord Brecon seemed to agree with him.

I wondered whether to keep the gun, but I made a mental note to be on the safe side and incorporate a new gun-cabinet in whatever plans I drew up for refurbishing the property. Otherwise, the arrangements seemed just what I needed. In fact, it all seemed too good to be true. On the other hand, I wondered how far from the straight and narrow I was prepared to stray. Did I mind using deception when claiming loans and grants? Did my intention to repay everything in due course make it all right? I comforted myself by dwelling on the thought that this was the way of the world.

As he drove us back to his 'old house' Lord Brecon said, "That looks satisfactory to me. The stables are in a better state than the house and I'll tell Foxy so. Of course, you must decide if you want to keep that farm, but I could just sweeten it a bit for you if you like."

"I'd love a sweetener. What do have in mind?"

"Well, if you were to let me keep my horses there and let Dai, my groom, have the caravan, I could pay you a little rent. And I'm sure Foxy would say the same if you found somewhere for one of his lads to stay and look after the 'resting' racehorses."

Johnny said, "Yeah! Count me in too!"

After I got back to Cardiff, I had a phonecall from Major Fox. "Lord Brecon's told me of your visit to the farm. I hope you keep it. Listen, Matt, I could persuade the others to count the value of the farm towards your payment into the syndicate. You see, if we buy a place, we won't get any grants or cheap loans like you could. It seems near enough to Chepstow and to my place to suit everyone. Nobody wants to have to move all the horses to somewhere across the Severn, least of all Lord Brecon or Johnny Whyte."

I talked things over with Esso and later, by phone, with his father. He said, "That sounds good. Not too much to do and plenty of scope. I like the sound of the cottages. You could let them out to tourists. Might have to be self-catering. But it'd bring in a bit of money and you can get grants for doing places up if it's for tourism."

Chapter 8

I went home for the Easter holidays and found Mother had lots of things to keep her busy, including sorting out the garden of the new house she had moved into and advising the wife of the new rector about some of the peculiarities of the parish. On Easter Saturday, I went into Salisbury and came upon Ruth. She said she was house-hunting and job-hunting, since she had to vacate the curate's house.

I said, "Let's talk. Fancy a coffee?"

She nodded. I began to head to *Ye Olde Tea Shoppe* which was nearby, but she said she'd rather go to MacDonald's. I was puzzled. When we sat down, she explained, "The staff at the tea shop hear everything and gossip to all their favourite customers. In here, nobody takes any notice. Besides, all these mums and kids are making enough noise to cover our conversation."

The coffee wasn't as good as in the other place, but I saw her point. She said, "I don't know what to do. Everyone seems to know all about Arnie. I feel as if they think I was covering up for him, but I wasn't. I still can't believe he was guilty. What if that newsagent was lying or mistaken? What if he did give those keys back to your father and he mislaid them?"

"How is Arnie?"

"Not good. He's in a state because he can't get any booze and is trying not to start on drugs, which people keep trying to sell him. He's also scared they'll find out he's a priest and give him a bad time."

"He doesn't want to use this as an opportunity to speak of his faith?"

"I don't think his faith is in a very good condition right now and he can hardly defend himself if things get physical, having only one arm, you know?"

I knew.

I got some more coffee for both of us. I asked, "Why not move to a new area? Somewhere nobody knows you? Make a fresh start?"

"I suppose it might help. Where?"

"I like Cardiff."

"I don't speak Welsh."

I laughed. "Neither do I, nor half the people in Cardiff. They say there are three languages in Cardiff and you can get by OK if you're fluent in any one of them. There's English, Welsh and Kairdiff. The last is the local dialect of English with bits of anglicised Welsh mixed in. I'm fluent in two of the three."

Ruth laughed. It made her face look different. I was glad, but sad for her that she was so unhappy most of the time.

She asked about my dilemma. I told her the latest. She said she was sorry but not sorry. I told her that Esso had said women were attracted by money. She said with a chuckle that she wished she had been. Then she asked about my love life. I felt awkward as I tried to explain.

"My pal Sam always seems to have loads of girlfriends. I'm friendly with a lot of girls, but I keep holding back. I think it's because I'm a Christian and I want it to mean something when I go to bed with a woman, even if we're not married or engaged. I feel it should be the start of something long-term. See what I mean?"

Ruth said, "That's how Arnie and I were. Hmm." She frowned and stared at her empty coffee cup. One MacDonald's cup is much like another, but she seemed to be studying it. Finally she said, "There's something nobody knows. I don't know if I should say anything to you, but I told your father because I trusted him. Now I hope I can trust you."

"Even if I'm not going to be a clergyman, I hope I can still be a Christian."

She held my hand. I felt a surge of excitement that was rather inconvenient at that time. She said, "Arnie and I were married just after he graduated from theological college. He was in his first curacy when he had that car accident and lost his arm. After that, even when he seemed to be back to normal in most respects – God! What do I mean 'Normal'? Anyway, whatever, he didn't regain his libido. I know it bothered him although I said it was OK and things take time, you know."

"I'm not surprised at what you say. Why are you troubled by it now?"

"I wonder if he tried it on with that awful woman and got mad when he couldn't make it. I wonder if there was something wrong with me that was putting him off when we were together. Perhaps he thought I was judging him? Or he just didn't fancy me any more?"

"That's silly. Wouldn't any other woman be more likely to judge? And that one who complained was a well-known troublemaker." I studied my cup for a minute before adding, "Surely, any man would fancy you – well, more than that woman, for sure."

"Thanks. I've always known you fancy me. It's OK – don't apologise. If things were different,,, but they're not. I'm still married and you're not looking for a bit of a fling. I think you're wise to wait for the right one. I hope she comes along soon."

As we left, I wondered what I meant about still being a Christian, when I was planning on making money by dubious means. Anyway, I would keep Ruth's secret. I also kept wondering about Arnie. Could Ruth be right and he was innocent? Could there be things the police hadn't discovered? I wished that could be so.

****

Back in Cardiff, I tried not to think about Arnie, and for a different reason not to think about Ruth. I made several attempts at seeing Liz, but between her studies and her racing she had little spare time, apparently. I was therefore pleased when I got a message from Izzy saying she would like to come to Cardiff for a weekend.

On Saturday Morning, I met her at the station and as we walked towards the shops in the St David's Centre and I took her on a slight detour and said, "Here's the famous rugby ground: Cardiff Arms Park."

"Isn't it called the Millenium Centre since, err… the Millenium?"

"That's what a lot of people think. It's true that for the Millenium, Wales created a grand new international stadium, which they called, unsurprisingly the Millenium Stadium, but now it's called the Principality Stadium because it's owned by the Principality Building Society – and NOT because it belongs to the principality of Wales. That's a sore point with some."

"Oh? Right. Then why did you call it Cardiff Arms Park? Are you living in the past – like the Church?"

"No. I forgot to say that the Arms Park is still here. Look! It's next to the Principality Stadium. Nowadays it's the home of Cardiff Rugby Club, where I go to watch them play every Saturday in the season, except when I'm playing for Cardiff University, which is quite often. Of course, some Saturdays I go to the races at Chepstow."

"I remember Esso saying you both played. I was amazed when I first met you. I always expect rugby players to be big strapping blokes like Esso."

"A lot are, especially the forwards, but I play scrum-half, which is a position for little nifty chaps like me."

"You must be tough! Surely you get shoved around by the big'uns?"

"I suppose I am fairly tough. I usually manage to hold my own against the big lumps. Of course, I've been playing rugby for a long time, so I'm used to it."

"Funny thing. You don't seem like a tough guy. But then, most of the really tough guys I've known didn't.

79

Unlike all the poseurs I keep meeting. Oh! Is that the castle down there? Esso says it's worth a visit."

I said, "I agree with Esso. Speaking of him, can we be clear about your relationship?"

"Well, he's my stepbrother and we get on OK but that's about it. Oh! Were you afraid you'd be treading on his toes? No? Oh, I get it. Do you think I'd be upset if I knew about his many girlfriends? No worries – he's not really my type in that way, but I'll be happy to see him while I'm in Cardiff."

"That's a relief. He told me that Zoe was coming for the weekend, before I told him you were coming too. Maybe we can go out as a foursome tonight?"

"As long as it's not the kind of foursome I've heard about with you rugger types."

When we reached the castle she was intrigued by the 'animal wall' where sculpted animals appeared to be climbing the lowest battlements onto the street. She was even more impressed on the guided tour when she saw the unusual mock-mediaeval décor and furnishings acquired in the eighteenth and nineteenth centuries by the Marquis of Bute. 'Bizarre' was the word some people have used. I like them, but wouldn't want my living-room decorated in such a way.

When the tour was over, Izzy said, "They didn't take us up to the high tower – Norman, isn't it? It is OK to go up there?"

It was OK but my taste for going up high towers had diminished since my father's death. However, I told myself my feelings were irrational and set out up the long flights of steps to the keep and then up the tower itself. Rationality did not prevent my nerves playing up to the extent that I was afraid I was going to be sick.

She enthused at the view. "Look at that! You can see England from here – and most of Wales. It's fantastic."

I agreed, but after that I was quiet as we made our way back down. I began to relax when we began exploring the grounds. Izzy asked me about my studies and my business ventures. After I told her, she said, "What's the matter? You don't seem excited at the idea you're gonna be a successful businessman."

"I'm not sure about getting into agriculture. I mean, I know nothing about it."

"Nobody's asking you to become a farmer. Be a businessman!"

We were about to leave the castle when she asked, "What's that building?"

"It's the only Roman part of the castle still standing. There's a museum inside it. Did you know they once found an inscription in Latin to someone called Didymus? They say he must have been one of the first governors of this city. Maybe that's how it got it's name."

"How?"

"In Welsh Cardiff is called 'Caerdydd' and it might once have been called 'Caer Didydd' – Welsh for 'The fortress of Didymus' – perhaps. Other ideas exist, but it's possible."

"Hmm. You're not just a pretty face, are you?"

"Flattery always works."

We waited for a bus to take us to somewhere near the flat I shared with Esso on Cathedral Road.

Izzy asked, "Did you go to a public school?"

"Yes. Not one of the well-known ones. Does it matter?"

"No, but it's surprising. You're not like most of the other public-school boys I've met."

"Just as I thought I was beginning to impress you with my erudition."

"That's not what I meant. Why do people send their children to public schools?"

"To get a good education. To impress people who are easily impressed? I expect that only works if the people you want to impress have heard of the school in question. What do you think?"

"You forgot to mention the good careers advice and personal contacts because a lot of the staff have got friends in high places."

"Hmm. I suppose so. It didn't occur to me because my family already had lots of contacts in various ecclesiastical places."

The bus came and we got on.

I said, "I see what you mean about public schools, but what is your point about me?"

"It's what public schools seem to do to their pupils. It's an attitude. Confidence. At its worst, it's arrogance, but a lot just have a quiet confidence that they're going to succeed no matter what they try to do. But you seem unsure of yourself."

"I was confident before. I mean, when I was sure I wanted to go into the Church. Since I've been doubting that, I've not been too sure what is the right thing for me."

When we got off the bus and began walking along Cathedral Road, Izzy said, "You know we both love history? Well, you must know there's two kinds of historians with two ways of looking at it."

"There are more than two. Which two were you thinking of?"

"One lot reckon it's all about trends: waves and troughs. Whatever happens is because summat else just happened first, you know?"

"Yes, I've heard that."

"But then there's this other lot that say bollocks to that. History's the story of great men. I'd say great women too, but never mind. What they mean is that the people who make history make things happen and stuff the trends and all that."

"I've heard that too. So what?"

"Are you gonna be one of the people that lets things happen to you or are you gonna go and make things happen?"

I thought about that as I let us into the flat. Indeed, I have thought about it a lot since. A I put the kettle on, I said, "I think there's another reason for my lack of confidence. There was one man, apart from some of my own relatives, that I really trusted and admired as a Christian. He was my father's curate. He's in jail now for murdering my father. I went to the trial. I really wanted him to be innocent. It had to be a mistake. But the evidence was there."

"So you don't trust anyone now?"

"I don't trust my own judgment."

"Maybe you were too trusting. Just accept that people aren't always what they seem and don't worry about it. Be like Brian! He doesn't let anyone put one over on him. He doesn't leave himself open. I'll bet you could do as well as him if you made your mind up. Believe in yourself!"

After that we concentrated on having a good time and succeeded.

Chapter 9

I focussed on my studies and revision until the end of term. I did well in my year-end exams and was confirmed in my place on the management course for the following academic year. Just before the exams I received the initial instalments of most of the grants and loans I had applied for and paid off my student loan, leaving enough in the bank for my fees and expenses for most of the following year. I was therefore feeling happy when I went home for the summer armed with a reading list to enable me to hit the ground running when I began my new course. I contacted each my new employees by e-mail to reassure them I was not going to interfere, but on the other hand I would not abandon them. They all seemed happy with what I said.

I was still feeling cheerful when Mother said, "Now you're home, would you mind popping down to the police station in Salisbury to collect your father's things – his personal effects, as they say? Now it's all over we can have them back. They told me weeks ago, but I keep putting it off. Take the car if you like."

I took the car. The sergeant fetched a cardboard box and laid its contents on the desk, handing me a printed list for me to check and sign. He said, "I know it says 'camera' but it doesn't say 'smashed to bits'. You can amend it if you like. I dunno if the thing's worth repairing or if you can use any of it for spares, but it's your property, or your mother's, I suppose, to do what you like with."

I checked the list to the objects in front of me. All present and correct. I almost asked him to put the remains of the camera in the bin, but thought I'd see if anyone we knew had any use for it. I wondered why the huge telephoto lens was detached, as Father always used it when photographing birds from the tower. It didn't seem to have broken off. Perhaps he was just changing lenses when he fell? No! That was most unlikely. Never mind.

Father's watch was amazingly undamaged. It wasn't working, but it might just need a new battery. His wallet was there, complete with credit cards and a twenty pounds in notes. There were also two rather worn pound coins. He seldom carried change unless he knew he was going to need it. He said it cluttered up his pockets. Obviously, he had not been robbed.

Three bunches of keys. On one ring was the key to the front door of the rectory, accompanied by the one to the back door. I would have to give those to the new rector. His car key was on its own fob. Then there was a big ring holding all the church keys. Wait a minute! Hadn't they been accounted for?

I signed the sheet and hurried home. I asked Mother how many sets of church keys she had managed to account for.

"Why, all of them dear. I asked all the keyholders and checked that Father's were in the drawer where he always kept them if he didn't expect to be needing them, which was most of the time, since the church was seldom locked completely, what with different people needing to go in and out. What? Why are you looking like that?"

"What about these? Father must have had them on him when he fell. That means Arnie wasn't lying when he said he'd handed his in. They must be the ones that were in the drawer."

"All, right! No need to get so worked up. It's only a bunch of... Oh! Oh God! I see. You mean, Arnie couldn't have got in by the external door to the tower. So he couldn't have killed Father, unless he'd gone through the church and nobody noticed?"

"Quite! And everyone there knew he'd been suspended and banned from setting foot in the place. They'd have said if they'd seen him."

We stood staring at each other. After a while, I said, "We'd better tell the police."

"Yes. I suppose so. Oh, dear. What a fool I must seem. To think that poor man is in prison because of my mistake. Mind you – what about Mrs Taylor at the newsagents? How come she saw Arnie there, when he swore he was at home?"

"I dare say you're not the only one capable of making a mistake!"

I found it hard to get anyone at the police station to take any interest. The detectives on the case were not based locally and the senior investigating officer was no longer based where he had been. I finally had an idea and went to see Father's solicitor. He was more than interested. He was angry. "The police should have known about the keys in his pocket and counted them along with the rest. That's what got them interested in Rev Armstrong. It was only after that that they found that woman who said she'd seen him near the church. Mind you, we've got to find out if she could have been mistaken, not that I think the poor fellow climbed up the outside of the tower."

He looked at his diary on his laptop. "Damn! I'm fully tied up all week. I'll phone the police and try to get things moving, but I'll have to rely on them reinterviewing Mrs Taylor."

I thanked him and left. I did not intend to rely on the police. I went back to Amesbury, to the newsagents. I waited until it was quiet before going in.

"Hello Matthew. Nice to see you again, how's your studies going?"

"Not bad. Passed my second-year exams OK but I'm changing my course next year."

"Well, I hope you do as well in your new subject, whatever it is."

"Thank you. Mrs Taylor, do you mind just going over what you remember about that day when my father was killed? I just want to be as clear as I can about it all in my own mind."

"You know I went all through it with the police and again in court?"

"Yes, I do. I just hope you won't mind setting my mind at rest about a few details, if you can remember them."

"I expect I can. That day's stuck in my mind. It was all such a shock, as it must have been for you and your poor mother."

I nodded. She went over everything I was familiar with. Then I asked, "What I can't help wondering is, if Rev Armstrong didn't actually come in, how can you be sure it was him? It's hard to make people out through the door, even when it's open, unless you're at that end of the shop."

"You are quite right. However, the gentleman he'd been talking to outside came in and apologised for tendering a fivepound note just for a newspaper, due to not having any change. He said he'd given all his pound coins to 'that vicar chap' for the car park, you see. I remember him saying he hoped he found a couple in good condition as most of them were well worn."

"So it might have been some other clergyman, my father even?"

"But your father was up on the tower. Everyone knows that, sadly. And how many other clergymen are there around here?"

"Do you remember what time this was?"

"Not exactly. It was before lunch and not first thing. We'd been open for some time."

"I see. This man didn't know who it was who asked for change? He didn't say his name or even say 'curate' or 'rector' – was he not local?"

"Well, I suppose he could see the dog-collar. He must have not done his coat right up."

"Do you know the man?"

"Well, no. The man's not from here. But I do see him from time to time. I don't know his name. I think he's a travelling salesman or something like that. Always polite and cheerful. Always wears a nice suit."

"Yes, well, I'd better not keep you any longer. Thank you. You've been very helpful."

I wondered if I could possibly find this salesman, or whatever he was. When I went home, I looked through Father's things again, starting with his wallet. I found a car park receipt dated the day in question at nine thirty in the morning. I told the solicitor what I had discovered. He said he would pursue it with the police. He also said, "I think I know the man you're looking for. He's an insurance broker. I've dealt with him at times. I'll contact him and ask if he can be more specific about the clergyman he saw that day. I say, have you got a photo of your father and one of Mr Armstrong? I'd like to get this chap to see if he recognises him."

"Yes. I've even got one of them together. You could ask which one he saw that day. I'll e-mail it to you. You might also ask if he noticed the man had only one arm. While you're at it, you might get the police to look a bit closer at the women who were cleaning the church when my father was killed. If any of them had a motive, they'd certainly have had the opportunity. I don't expect the others would've noticed one slipping out and up the tower."

"Hmm. I see your point. I can only suggest it informally and hope they follow it up."

I went to see Ruth. When I told her about the latest developments, she burst into tears and hugged me. When she was composed, I said, "I want to see Arnie to apologise for doubting him."

She said, "I'm sure you don't need to, we all know how the evidence looked, but I'll let him know when I go to see him, in a couple of days, and I'll let you know if it's OK. If you like, I'll send you an e-mail with the link so you can arrange a visit through the prison service."

"Thanks."

"What? Is there something else on your mind? You look worried."

"Now everyone knows Arnie's innocent, but who's guilty? I've tried to think who could have wanted to kill my father and who had the opportunity. Nobody comes into both categories, but I can think of one with a motive who seems pretty nasty."

"I can't."

"What about the woman who accused Arnie of molesting her? My father stuck up for Arnie and did his best to get the complaint rejected by the diocese. Killing him and letting Arnie take the blame would have suited her and she was known to be a serial liar."

"Surely not? Making false accusations is a long way from murder."

"Yes, I suppose so. Oh – what about her husband? What if he believed her and was mad at Arnie and at therefore at Dad? I heard he had a nasty side to him."

"I heard that too, but nasty isn't the same as being a murderer."

"What if he went to confront my father and got into a row which got out of hand?"

"I hadn't thought. But neither of them had access to the tower."

"Most of the time, when any murderer is caught, lots of people say they'd never have believed it, he was such a nice chap and so on. I mean, sorry, but I felt like that about Arnie for a time, may God forgive me."

"I'm sure God and Arnie both forgive you."

The next day, I studied the documentation regarding grants and loans again and realised I needed to do at least something in the real world rather than just on paper – or online. This was partly to appease my conscience, which had never quite gone away, and partly so I would have something to show any auditors who chose to check on my business. I found an architect specialising in renovating and modernising agricultural properties and invited him to visit the farm with a view to producing a plan. He gave me a date in the following week and I agreed to meet him on site and packed a few things so I could stay in one of the potential holiday cottages for a few days. I wanted to spend some time there before the man came, so I could think about what I wanted to do and to stay on a little afterwards to reflect on the architect's recommendations.

I saw a missed call on my phone. It was from Ruth. I called her. "Hi, Ruth, is it about the prison visit?"

"Not exactly. Arnie's in hospital. He's tried to kill himself with a massive overdose of cocaine."

I couldn't think of anything to say. She said, "Are you there?"

"Yes. Sorry! Just trying to take it in. Can I visit him in the prison hospital?"

"No. There's no point. He's in a coma. And he's not in the prison hospital. They've transferred him to the general so he can get more specialist care. Oh God! This is getting worse all the time."

I couldn't disagree. I told Mother. She invited Ruth to come to the church's weekly prayer-meeting. She assured her the others present would not judge either her or Arnie but would be supportive. I obviously had to go too. It felt strange, as we prayed for Arnie. I found myself saying the same sort of prayers the others were praying, unsurprisingly. It was not that I didn't mean what I said: I certainly wanted Arnie to recover and to be released from prison. I wanted him to be restored to the priesthood – if he still wanted to be.

What felt wrong was that I was no longer sure that I believed in the deity in whom everyone else had such faith. My faith had been damaged, as they would have seen it. Others might say it had been broadened and that my concept of God was less like a person, more of a force that could encompass other religions and non-religious philosophies. I realised that the one I sort of believed in was less of a comfort when you prayed for someone at death's door.

After the meeting, Ruth said she had found it a big encouragement and thanked everyone. I felt guilty for feeling a touch superior to these simple folk with their traditional concept of God. Of course, I had hidden my thoughts, more from a desire to avoid giving offense than for any nobler principle.

The next day I phoned the hospital only to be told they couldn't tell me anything about Arnie over the phone. Then I phoned Ruth who said the hospital had told her his condition was stable and they didn't expect any change for several days. I decided to go to the farm and keep in touch with Ruth, Mother and Jan by phone and online.

Chapter 10

I hired a car from a firm in Salisbury and drove to the farm, where Ivan the stable lad gave me a somewhat surly welcome before asking me to help with the horses' feeds and turnout. I thought he had a cheek, but I enjoyed the contact with the horses. I found it impossible to tell the two chestnuts one from another. Likewise the two bays. After some hesitation, I asked Ivan. He showed me a plait he had put in the mane of one chestnut and also one of the bays to save himself the trouble of examining each of them in great detail to avoid mistakes. It mattered because they were on slightly different diets, some being more prone to putting on too much weight than others.

I said he must be grateful that Silver was so easy to identify. He sneered and said he was far from easy to keep clean as every speck showed on his white coat. I asked if it mattered when he was not going to be racing for months. Ivan pointed out that Johnny Whyte had the habit of asking for him to appear at photo opportunities at short notice and wanted him to look his best. Well, Johnny was paying the bills, so nobody was going to complain. Except Ivan.

I began to go through every room in the farmhouse and all over every outbuilding, making notes and rough sketches. I walked around the outside, thinking about potential extensions. Unlike Ivan, Dai, Lord Brecon's groom, was pleasant and cheerful. On my second day, he came to me and said, "Listen, see, I know I don't even work for you, like, but I hope you don't mind if I ask you a favour."

"You can ask!"

"Right, well, what it is, see, I got a hospital appointment tomorrow in Newport. No – don't worry, I'm not very ill, but it's summat I've been trying to get sorted for ages and it keeps getting put back, only this time it's not and guess what – the farrier's coming tomorrow and I don't wanna put him off, because he's a bit funny like. You know, hates being messed around. Of course, it's OK if he messes us around like, isn't it?"

"What's the favour you're asking?"

"Ah, yes, well, what it is, he always wants someone to hold the horses for him while he's shoeing them. Says you can't just tie them up in case they pull back hard and do themselves a mischief, like. Well, it turns out I've nobody else I can ask this time what'll be around all day. Not that the shoeing's gonna take all day, is it? I mean, there's only his lordship's old hunter, his new hunter and the Welsh cob. He's coming at nine, so he should be gone before lunchtime, even if he takes his time. Should be a piece of cake as long as you weren't planning on going away for much of the day. I'd not half be grateful, mind. If I can do anything for you, just let me know, isn't it?"

"OK. I'll do it."

"Great! Oh, there's one other thing. Well, it's nothing really, but there's a cheque already made out to the farrier from his lordship. All you gotta do is give it to the man once the job's done. You don't mind, do you?"

"No. That'll be fine."

I continued with my survey of the buildings. I was enjoying thinking of the sorts of improvements the buildings could take. I spent the evening making more sketches as new ideas occurred to me.

I was having breakfast at eight the next morning when there was a knock at the door as if someone was trying to smash through it. I blearily opened it and felt a blast of cold, damp air while I saw a well-built man of average height. He was probably in his thirties and either prematurely bald or had shaved his head. "Are you this Matthew Chaplain that's looking after the hunters today?"

"Err, yes, sort of. What can I do for you?"

"Do? You can shift yourself and come and let me get on with the shoeing. That's what!"

I put some shoes on and a coat before following him to the stableblock. The farrier led the old bay hunter out of his stable and cursed on seeing his feet needed picking out where he had been standing in muck and shavings all night. I had hoped Dai would have attended to that sort of thing before he left. On the other hand, if the shoes were coming off, wouldn't most of the compacted items fall away with little help from anyone? The farrier took a lot of time making all the feet clean enough to his satisfaction before starting to remove the worn shoes. After that, things went smoothly. The horse stood peacefully, seeming bored rather than anxious at every stage, making me wonder why I was needed. I had hoped to use the time to run my building plans through my mind, but was distracted by the farrier's constant moaning about the weather, the state of the roads, the government and the unreasonableness of several of his clients.

The younger hunter was a handsome grey. He was a bit more jittery than the bay and the farrier's bad temper and impatience did nothing to calm him. I had to use all my charm to persuade the animal to cooperate, which I found surprisingly exhausting.

The cob was as easygoing as the bay and the shoeing got off to a good start. However, after a few minutes, the farrier cursed, stood up straight and said, "This foot's sore. That's because he's been ridden too much with a loose shoe. Do you know how much they intend to ride him at the moment?"

"I've no idea. Why?"

"Why? Because ideally, he wants a good rest. If they're gonna keep on riding him the way they seem to have been, he'll be lame soon."

"Perhaps you should ask Lord Brecon."

"Don't be daft! You can never get hold of him. In one meeting after another, it seems."

He studied the foot again and finally said. "Tell you what I can do. I can put a bit of a leather pad under the shoe and use slightly lighter shoes. How's that?"

"I can't say. He's not my horse. If you can't contact Lord Brecon, I suppose you'd better do what you think is best."

"I'll have to take off the two shoes I've put on him already and put thin ones on those two feet or else he'll be uneven, see?" I saw. He sighed twice and cursed again before getting back to work. I was relieved when it was all over. Well, almost all. I went back to my cottage and fetched the cheque Dai had left.

"No! That's no good. You'll need to pay extra for the corrective shoeing on the cob. As it is, it's taken me longer than it should because I had to reshoe them two feet, like I said."

"I'm sorry, but this is the cheque Lord Brecon's groom left with me. I can't amend it. I suggest you take the matter up with lord Brecon. Or you could just add the extra to your next bill, if you tell Dai to tell his employer."

"Are you trying to be funny? I haven't got time to go chasing owners for money. Anyone that doesn't pay up doesn't get my services again. You can take that up with his lordship."

"If I pay you the difference, can you give me a receipt so I can get the money back off Lord Brecon?"

"You're an awkward customer, aren't you? What a waste of time."

"Do you want the money or not?"

"Oh, all right. Cash only mind. I'm not taking a cheque from you, when I don't know you." I was thinking we had got to knowing each other pretty well that morning, but I found the cash and got a receipt.

I had a very late lunch and got back to going around all the buildings and making plans.

On the third day, I shared my thoughts with the architect and listened to his, making more notes. He promised to send me a report with recommendations and estimates along with an invoice for his initial fee. He may have misinterpreted my smile. I was glad to have something to show any lender or grant-making body should they get curious. I planned to take my time deciding what I wanted and more time implementing the ideas. Hopefully, I would be spending the money at a slower rate than it would come in.

Ruth phoned and said Arnie was out of danger, although still in hospital, and his solicitor had said he would be released on parole pending an appeal based on the new evidence he and I had pushed in front of the police. She said she had told Arnie how much I had done for him and he was anxious to thank me in person. I was just glad for them and said I would come and see them as soon as they let me know it was convenient.

I was getting ready to go home, trying to ignore the sound of Ivan arguing with someone on his phone, when a small but top-of-the-range four-by-four drove into the yard. Liz stepped out. We were both amazed at this meeting as nobody had told either of us what was happening. She came into my kitchen and we sat drinking coffee as she explained, "Major Fox asked me to come to the farm regularly to ride Silver and keep him fit."

"Why? He's not racing for ages."

"I know, but this is partly so he won't look fat in any photos with Johnny, but also because they want me to go hunting on him in the autumn, just before the National Hunt racing season starts."

"Why? But hunting's been banned for years now."

"They want me to ride him in a few hunter-chases. They think he's made for it. And they don't hunt anything nowadays, but we'll be riding with draghounds, which have always been legal and ethical. Johnny wouldn't want to be associated with real hunting – no way!"

"Will you be staying here?"

"That was the idea, but if it's a problem…"

"It's fine! I'm going home today, so you can move in here. Give me a ring if there's anything I need to know. Enjoy your riding. Silver really is a lovely horse."

Chapter 11

"I don't believe it!" I shouted. I was with Arnie and Ruth in their home. He was not looking well, but he was obviously much recovered from his overdose. She was still looking stressed, and for good reason. On top of everything, they had just been instructed to vacate their home because a new curate had been appointed to the church and, although still a priest, Arnie was without a job – a *living* as they say. The complaint of sexual misconduct had been upheld and his suspension extended, apparently indefinitely.

Ruth said, "Remember when I was househunting and jobhunting? Unfortunately, nothing came of it and I was too distracted by Arnie's hospitalisation to continue."

Arnie said, "Och! It's not that bad. I think the archdeacon will persuade folks to let us stay here a wee bit longer, but the new man will have to go into digs until we move out."

"Funnily enough, I may be able to help you. It's not much, and it's not in a good location if you're looking for work, but it might do for a bit. It's a farm cottage that'll be let for self-catering holidays when it's been done up a bit."

He asked, "How can you be sure they'll let us have it?"

"Because I sort of... err... own it." I found myself telling them the whole story, although I didn't exactly admit that I had made untrue statements in my grant and loan applications.

Arnie stared at me for a minute before saying, "Well, I knew you were thinking of a change of direction and I suppose it makes sense, but it's a wee bit of a shock. Anyway, Ruth and I will be very grateful if you really can let us move in there soon, whatever state it's in. I need time to think and pray about my future. These few months have given me a lot to think about." I could see that they would.

I had just got home when Major Fox phoned. "Are you still at the farm? I heard you were there."

"No. I'm at home in Amesbury, but I'm going down again soon. Not for long, but if there's anything..."

"Right! Well this is a bit tricky. I'm desperate for someone to look after the horses there, just for a bit, I hope. Ivan's quit. Bloody fool! Leaves the end of the week. Won't take an increased paypacket for an answer."

"What's got into him?"

"Bloody Brexit – that's what! Now we've left the EU he can't stay indefinitely unless he gets settled status and I've told him he's bound to get it but he says he's applied months ago and has answered all their damn fool questions and they don't seem satisfied. I know I filled in something saying he'd a job here and a good chance of something better if he stuck at it and I told him I'd write to them but he won't listen. It's panic stations."

"We haven't left yet. We're in a sort of halfway stage, aren't we? He's got months to sort it all out."

"Quite! Trouble is, some pal of his has been given his marching orders but he was in a totally different situation. No job. Nothing to prove he was here before whatever deadline they set. Ivan says he's heard all about that Windrush affair and doesn't trust the British Government. He wants to get out now. I think he's got a job in Poland. Of course, it hasn't helped that some fools have given him a bad time. You know, saying his sort are either scroungers or stealing our jobs. For God's sake! Whose job's he stolen? You can't get decent stable lads for love or money round here."

I waited for him to run out of breath before I said, "You mean you want me to go to the farm and look after your horses for while?"

"That's it! Look – if it helps, I'll pay you. Could even give you the odd tip so you can make a packet. What do you say?"

"I suppose I could stay there and get on with setting up my business and doing my studies and have time to do the horses too. Would it be OK if I rode one?"

"I forgot you said you could ride. All right. I'll let you have a saddle and bridle."

"I'll go down there the day after tomorrow and look after the horses until you get a full-time lad."

Arnie and Ruth hired a furniture van to take all their possessions to the farm. Only about half fitted into the cottage. The rest went into one of the outbuildings. We covered everything with waterproof sheets as the roof was prone to leaks. I drove the van back and hired a cheap four by four which I drove straight back to the farm. I had to spend one night on the sofa in the cottage Arnie and Ruth had moved into. The next day Ivan left and I moved into his cottage, which Ruth helped me clean.

"What's that doing here?" asked Ruth, pointing at the shotgun, propped in a corner.

"It's mine. The previous owner of the farm gave it to me, saying I'd probably need it. I let Ivan borrow it, as he enjoys a bit of shooting."

"Shouldn't it be in a locked cabinet?"

"I mean to have one made when I get round to it."

"At least keep it out of sight."

After some haggling, I put it in a cupboard in my kitchen, along with the few boxes of cartridges Ivan had not used.

Ruth and Arnie both offered to help me with the horses, but were nervous around them at first. Fortunately, Silver soon calmed them with his gentle manner.

After a couple of days, Ruth had become organised enough to cook for us all. I was going to provide some wine before realising how inappropriate that would be. After the meal, Arnie said, over coffee, "One wee thing bothers me. I mean, apart from all sorts of things. The doctors said it was a miracle I pulled through."

Ruth said, "Yes, it was an answer to all the prayers we kept praying for you." I felt awkward, remembering how little faith I had in a personal God who intervened like that.

The next day, Arnie was struggling to groom Silver, a task particularly difficult for someone with only one hand, but he refused to let me help him, saying he

needed to pull his weight. I said, "If you wish. But I really
don't mind if you just take it easy for a bit. And you can
start by letting me pick this horse's feet out. That's a job
that really does require two hands. You can carry on
brushing him.""

"That's kind of you, but I feel so bad about the
problems I've caused for you and Ruth and a lot of other
folk."

"You didn't kill my father. Whoever did is the one
who's made problems for all of us."

"Aye. I suppose you're right."

"Why do you not seem convinced?"

"Och! It's not just you and Ruth and people I've
let down. It's God."

"How?"

"You must know what I mean. I turned to drink
instead of to God when that woman accused me of
assaulting her and then I turned to drugs in prison. I could
think of nobody but myself all the time and was too scared
to admit I was a clergyman because of what the other
prisoners might do to me. I never tried to offer the Lord's
help to anyone."

I put down a hoof I had just picked out and stood
up to take a breath before starting on the next one as I said,
"I think you're being too hard on yourself. Priests are only
human. I should know. Remember what sort of family I
come from."

"Aye, but do you think your father would have
been proud of me?"

106

"Even when I was little, I sometimes overheard my father counselling colleagues who were going through hard times, even things they'd brought upon themselves. He said God was always in the business of forgiveness and second chances – even for curates!"

Arnie moved around to brush the other side of the horse. "You sound like your father – and that's a compliment."

We walked in silence to the field and turned Silver out. When we returned, Ruth joined us and we began filling haynets. Arnie said, "There's one thing that puzzles me. That is why I was as ill as all that. The doctors said I'd enough dope in me to put an elephant to sleep. Well, I know I wasnae trying to kill myself. At one time, I had thought of it but decided it was against what little faith I had left. I started taking drugs because I couldnae get hold of any drink in there, but I always took just enough to make me feel better. I suppose I could have taken an overdose by mistake, but I dinna remember possessing that much stuff."

I asked, "Do you think someone could have given you another dose while you were sort of out of it? Or switched it for a a more concentrated dose?"

"Why? That stuff costs money."

Ruth said, "When Arnie told me about that, I wondered if someone wanted to kill him."

He shook his head. "Again, why? I hadnae made any enemies inside as far as I could tell and I was no threat to anyone."

After that, Ruth made some coffee. When we were drinking it, Arnie said, "You know, there's another thing that bothers me. Who killed your father? The police have got nowhere, according to my solicitor. They havenae found anyone with a motive and they have no idea how anyone could have got into that tower without being noticed by the people working in the church, including your mother. Whatever they say, somebody must have done it."

Ruth flicked her hair off her face and said, "Now you've been cleared – or will be once the appeal is heard – does it matter?"

I thought I agreed with her, but Arnie said, "Aye! Surely, it matters that someone is getting away with killing the rector?"

I said, "Yes. I suppose I was so concentrating on the matter of your guilt or innocence that I lost sight of the bigger question. Now you've got me thinking about it, it's maddening that we don't know where to start."

For the rest of the day I kept thinking about that, going over everything I knew and a lot I didn't and came to no worthwhile conclusion.

The next day, I found that the hunting saddle Liz used for Silver fitted Red Heat and his apparent identical twin, Space Station. I rode Space first. He was a handful. Our ride was short. After a rest to calm my nerves, I rode Red. What a relief! He was so laid back and obedient to the bit.

Jan phoned me.

"Have you really got Grandad's farm?"

"Yes. I'm there now."

"Could I come and see it. What I mean is, could Bess and I come and ride there?"

"Why not? There are some other horses here, but if they bother her, we can put her in another field. There are some nice rides around here. Wait! Is Mum happy about this?"

It went quiet. I thought I'd upset her, but a minute later, I heard our mother's voice on Jan's phone. "You'd be doing me a favour. The girl doesn't know what to do with herself and I'm up to my neck in things. How many weeks can she stay with you? Ten?"

We laughed. I replied, "How about two for starters and see how it goes."

I persuaded Major Fox to collect Bess and Janice on his way back from the races and make a detour to my farm. Everyone laughed when the huge horsebox, designed to transport eight racehorses, disgorged one Shetland pony as well as one rather small thirteen-year-old girl. The travelling head lad handed me a saddle saying it would fit either of the two bays, adding that 'the guv'ner' would be very pleased if I could give them both some exercise if I had time.

We managed to take a spare bed, belonging to Arnie and Ruth, out of the barn and into their cottage. They agreed to supervise Janice when I was not doing so.

To everyone's surprise, the racehorses found themselves being bossed around by the Shetland. Apparently size is less important than attitude among horses.

Janice loved accompanying me when I exercised Red Heat. I was worried about going out on Space Station with Janice in case of mishaps, but the presence of the smaller animal seemed to calm the racehorse and we had another good ride.

The next day, Liz arrived again. This time she alerted me by text about an hour before. I told Ruth we needed to accommodate another visitor and she said she could provide bedding if I could find a bedroom with a bed. After a brief panic, I thought of the room above the stables that Ivan had vacated. Once that was settled, I introduced Liz to all my other guests. Ruth said she would like to invite Liz to dine with her and Arnie but hadn't got enough food for me and Janice as well. Liz said she would get us all a Chinese takeaway and phoned our orders to somewhere she apparently knew.

Over dinner, which was as good as Liz had predicted, we all updated each other as to who we were and why we were there.

When we were alone, I asked Liz, "What about you and Johnny? Are you... an item?"

"That's what everybody wants to know. I've promised not to tell. It's the mystery that keeps people interested. That and my spat with Zig-zag."

"Yes. I saw that on social media. Do you two not get on?"

"We're OK. The spat makes us more interesting."

"I thought you were both interesting. Anyway, is Zig-zag male or female? I don't know how to speak to or about him – or her. I mean, they say people like that prefer to be referred to as 'they' although it's not grammatically correct, as it's really a plural. They obviously don't like being called 'it' but they don't want to be defined by their gender."

Liz asked, "Have you never met someone like that before?"

"No. Not really, but I don't mind being defined by my gender. Do you?"

She wriggled her hips. "Is that a proposition?"

"Do you want it to be?"

"I'll think about it!"

The next day, as I was saddling Forest Oak, Liz began to get Silver ready for a ride. She said, "I know we don't want to go flat out, but I'd like to give Silver a bit of a run today. It wouldn't hurt to let Forest open up a bit too, but I don't think the Shetland can keep up. I don't want to overtax the pony."

Janice put her head over Bess's stable door. "How about letting me ride one of the big ones? I have ridden other horses apart from Bess, you know."

We let her ride Silver around the yard and the small paddock. Everything went well. Liz said, "You can come with us on him. We can ride Forest and Red. They'll go steadily enough. The other two are a bit less predictable, so we'll ride those when you're not with us. In fact you could ride Bess on your own, since you know your way around by now."

Liz was right. We gave the three racehorses a slow gallop at one stage of our ride. After that, we had no rest before going out again. I rode Red and Liz rode Dark Sea.

I was glad of her company, as she showed me a few tricks for steadying them when they got excited.

When we got back, Janice was putting Bess back into her stable. She said, "I enjoyed our gallop but it's fun in a different way when I'm riding Bess alone, just me and her. Thanks you two."

The tractor made its presence felt as it roared into the yard. As it came to a halt, Owain jumped out and said, "There's a fence come down in the top field where I've been growing corn. It'll take two of us, at least, to fix it. I know you're not a proper farmer like old Hugh, and he said if I needed any work doing I should ask you for permission to ring a bloke in the village that does all kinds of work."

"OK – if it needs doing, get him to do it and send the bill to the accountant. That's what we agreed with Hugh Evans."

"Right. Well, the thing is, I rang Bryn Jones – that's the guy I was telling you about – and he can't come for a couple of days. I don't wanna leave it that long, else them sheep'll be down off the tops and eat all the corn that's growing there. Even a temporary repair would be a help if you can manage to gimme a bit of a hand."

I sighed and sat on the trailer on which he had put the timbers and wire he intended to use, as well as a pile of tools. It was a bumpy ride even over fairly level ground.

Four of the Herefords were in the field. Before evicting them we walked along the fence and found it was broken on the side of the field that bordered their field as well as on the far side. We took some lengths of rope from the trailer and made makeshift halters with which we led them back to their field. They offered little resistance, but moved at their own pace – slow!

After we had done a running repair on the break in that stretch of fencing, Owain and I went to the side by the hill where the sheep grazed. I held the posts while he hit them. Then I held them while he stapled wire to them. After that, I helped unroll wire mesh and held it in place while he attached it to the strands of wire and to the posts.

I was just thinking we had done a satisfactory job, when Owain said, "That'll keep the sheep off for a day or two until Bryn can get here and do a proper job. Thanks." I was annoyed that I was going to have to pay someone to do a job I thought I had just done, but I supposed Owain knew what he was talking about. Then he said, "I don't believe it. It didn't take them long did it?"

I looked where he was pointing. A dozen sheep had found their way into the cornfield. We had just fenced them in. Owain phoned the sheep farmer who promised to come as soon as possible, with his dog, to move the mini flock. I helped Owain open up the fence. Why had I ever imagined farming could be a mere investment? If I had invested in shipping, I wouldn't have had to go to sea, surely?

Chapter 12

I was beginning to find it easier to tell the horses one from another by minor blemishes that were not obvious at first. What distinguished them more was their different characters. Space Station was always keen and fiery. Red Heat, on the other hand, was laid back and a much easier ride, except that he usually put in a quick buck when I turned him out into the field: something I had seen him do when his jockey first mounted. I had had difficulty staying in the saddle sometimes, but gradually got used to it. Both the bays, Dark Sea and Forest Oak, usually obeyed their rider, but the latter could be somewhat lazy for a racehorse, whilst his companion was always ready for gallop.

I began to reflect on their performance on the track. Some of their inconsistencies puzzled me. When she was back, I asked Liz what she thought. She said they all had their off days, like humans, but I felt there was more to it.

I was preparing to go back to Cardiff to begin my management studies course. The horses would soon be going back to the major's racing stables. I told Arnie and Ruth they were welcome to stay at the farm until they decided their next move. They could look after a few flat-race horses taking their Winter holidays as well as Bess, as Lord Brecon's groom didn't want to have any more horses to look after apart from his hunters.

Arnie said, "I'm glad I've been able to stay here. It's been peaceful and I've been able to think and pray about my situation."

"Have you heard anything from the church authorities?"

"Not yet. But I'm not sure if it matters."

"Are you doubting your faith or your calling?"

"Not my faith. As to my calling, it's a question of what God is calling me to."

"You mean you might not be called to the priesthood?"

"Mmm well... I went through a phase of thinking God had abandoned me, but gradually I began to wonder if it was just that he was trying to show me something. I saw some pretty awful things while in prison. I think I'd like to do something to improve things."

"Prison reform?"

"Aye! That's one idea. I've been in touch with some charities and pressure groups to see how I might fit in. Of course, if I do get reinstated to the priesthood, I could be a prison chaplain. There's scope there for doing good."

"I think there's a prison chaplain in my family. Perhaps you'd like to meet him?"

"Aye – please! But there's something else. I wasnae the only one inside who was innocent. A lot of them had had very poor legal representation. Some did not even know they had a right to appeal. Then there were some who'd done nothing wrong. Or nothing much. Yet they'd had the book thrown at them."

115

Ruth twisted a lock of hair in her fingers as she said, "You know, I'm so glad you've overcome your bitterness and all that and can perhaps see how God might use your experience for good. I mean, a lot of the people you met in prison never had your education or any sort of chance in life. I know, because I met some other prisoners' wives and girlfriends. I've been thinking whether we could do anything for them."

Arnie said, "Aye. I recall you told me about the wife of another prisoner who'd got life for a murder he insists he didnae commit."

"Yes. She said she wished he had committed it. He'd have been out sooner."

I asked, "How can that be?"

She said, "Well, you know, every time he tells anyone he's innocent – not the other prisoners, but the parole board, the psychiatrist or even the chaplain – well, they say he's not showing any remorse. Of course, he won't go to a session with the victim's family because he knows they'll expect him to say sorry."

Arnie said, "I do know that some pretend to be sorry just so as to get parole. The powers that be dinna like it if you're saying the police, the courts, the jury and everyone got it wrong, but we know they sometimes do. Of course some people have no scruples and can be good liars. But I wouldnae say sorry for a crime I didnae commit and I couldnae show remorse. I'd feel phoney. I canna be the only one."

I said, "As you both feel this way, I can see you could do a lot of good working for a charity or something, whether you've got your collar back to front or not."

Ruth looked intently at me and said, "You know that chat you had with Arnie a little while ago about not beating himself up? Well, it was really helpful. I mean, I can tell, and I think you really could be a good vicar, just like your father."

Arnie said, "Aye. What you said didnae sound like stuff you'd read or heard in a lecture. It came from inside. It really was a big help."

I was surprised. It made me think again about my plans for changing my career. Was being a chaplain in my blood?

Arnie said, "We'd like to stay here a wee bit longer. We enjoy looking after the horses and we cannna make any serious plans until I know if I'm going to be restored to the priesthood. Even if I don't go back to parish work, it might be helpful in some other ministry."

"I'm glad you said that. I was wondering if I could get a reliable groom before I go back to uni. Please stay as long as you like."

I felt guilty about wanting only to make money and about my negative reaction to the church's failings when Arnie had suffered so much yet was determined to turn it to good. However, I was enjoying reading about management and was looking forward to the course. I had studied my own finances and estimated how much I could afford for improvements to the farm: enough to keep the lenders and grant-givers happy for a while. I would have

enough over to pay my tuition fees and to live on in
Cardiff next term. I might even have some left.

I called the major and negotiated a share in the
syndicate which took into account my purchase of the
farm. He was delighted. Then he said, "You know, I've
been thinking Red would be good in Hunter Chases, but
I've nobody to take him hunting to get him qualified. Liz
tells me you've been riding him and got on OK. Even
popped a few jumps. You could hunt him for me if you
like." I was thrilled, although somewhat anxious as to how
I would fare riding a steeplechaser in the hunting field.
However, Liz assured me everything would be fine and
we travelled together with her father's groom, Dai, in a
horsebox containing Red and Silver as well as Lord
Brecon's hunter.

The meet was held in the grounds of Caerphilly
Castle, one of the biggest in Europe, with a leaning tower
making it as distinctive, but not as famous, as Pisa. Lord
Brecon, Johnny and the major met us at the meet. As ever,
Johnny stood out in white and was much photographed.
He said, "I'm thinking of having some more riding lessons
and coming hunting with you in the not-too-distant
future."

Major Fox commented, "I hope you know the
correct dress code for draghunting? Look at all these
people." I hoped he was not looking at me, as, although I
had bought the correct protective headgear, I had had to
make do with a tweed coat which I had borrowed, and
some cheap(ish) riding boots and off-white jodhpurs. At

least I didn't stick out like a sore thumb. Liz looked as if she was in her natural habitat, just as her father did.

Once the hunt began, I rode as close to Liz as possible for moral support. This proved a good move, as Red seemed happy to keep with Silver and not overtake the rest. He also avoided the cardinal sin of kicking hounds, which another horse committed resulting in his rider's being ordered to go home.

I found the hunt exhilarating once I overcame my fear and began to trust my horse. At one stage, we were cantering through a field when I noticed a fox watching us from the shelter of the hedge to my right. Once the hounds and the first few riders had passed, he cheekily trotted across the field, risking getting trampled by some of the horses, although none seemed to take any notice of him. Lord Brecon and Liz laughed at the thought of having to explain how we came to kill a fox while out draghunting.

The next time I went hunting the meet was in the grounds of a country house hotel near Rogerstone. Johnny rode Silver accompanied by Liz on her father's grey hunter, while Lord Brecon rode his old bay. He laughed when he saw Johnny was in correct hunting kit except that everything he wore was white. This attracted a lot of attention, not all of it apparently sympathetic, but the master ruled it was acceptable. I wondered what conversations had taken place beforehand. When hounds were set on the artificial scent and began running, Liz's mount became more excited and hard to control than either of our racehorses and I gained a new respect for her horsemanship (or is it horsewomanship?).

Johnny thoroughly enjoyed himself and bought drinks for all the hunt followers at the hotel afterwards. Someone asked him what was his favourite drink to which he replied, "A snowball, of course!"

I enjoyed going draghunting with Liz for a few more Saturdays at the beginning of the new academic year and then watched when somebody else rode Red in a few hunter chases. Several members of the syndicate told me they made more money from betting than from prizemoney. I wondered why we were always more successful than most punters. Still, I wasn't complaining.

****

In late October, Jan sent me an e-mail with a lot of photos attached. I was still studying them when she phoned. "I took Dad's camera to school and got the photography club to help me extract the photos from the SIM card. Some didn't come out but I've sent you and Mum all the ones that did. Not bad, eh?"

I was delighted and couldn't thank her enough. She asked, "Who's the guy in the distance? And why did he try to hide from the camera?"

When she directed me to the right photo, I stared at it for a long time. The photo was of a bird but a man was visible in the background although out of focus. He was in several photos, apparently taken in rapid succession. He was staring at the camera in one, holding his hands to his face in another and turning away in a third.

I said, "Some people don't like having their photo taken. Not everyone is like Johnny Whyte!"

After an unusually long silence for her, she said, "Do you think that man had something to hide? Something bad enough to be a motive for murder?"

I said, "Unfortunately, even if it was him, we can't tell who he was, he's out of focus. And we don't know how he could have got up the tower without anyone seeing him go into the church."

Janice said, "I'll bet the police could find out who he was, if they tried. They've got all sorts of hi-tech stuff to do that. If only we could get them to open up the case."

"I wish we could, but how? If the photo was a bit clearer, we might get them interested, but as it is…"

Sometimes the answer to a problem is so obvious you don't see it until it hits you. This one hit me just then. I said, "I think I know a man who can. Esso! He works for a very advanced hi-tech company that investigates cybercrime. If he used their equipment, he might be able to enlarge the photo and maybe improve the focus."

When I asked Esso, he said, "The firm I work for do have some pretty advanced equipment, and I think I can get them to do this as a favour. They might want to talk to you about why it's so important. I know I can tell them but, let's face it, it is a bit unusual."

"OK."

A few days later, I went to the races at Chepstow and to a party in a nearby hotel hosted by Johnny Whyte. I escorted Izzy, who was impressed by my apparent entrepreneurial skill. Most of my achievements were due to the advice of her stepfather, Brian, but I let her give me some of the credit.

Major Fox was there, which gave me a chance to ask him about something that had been bothering me. I waited for the right moment, hoping neither of us would consume so much alcohol as to prevent a serious conversation. It looked as if I was going to be unlucky, but quite late in the evening, I heard him say, "Listen, Johnny, can you hang on a minute? I'll show you and Zigzag what I mean. I've got a book of roadmaps in my car."

I followed him to the car park and said, I had a question for him. He hovered, keys in hand next to his Mercedes. "Can't it wait until we're back inside?"

"You might want to keep this conversation confidential."

"All right - go on!"

I said, "I can tell Red Heat from Space Station. Remember I looked after them both at my farm in Summer and I hunted Red. Please don't argue. I know. I know you sometimes swap them around. They usually lose when you do that, because of their different personalities."

"Well, you know, horses are no more consistent in their behaviour than people are. Otherwise, there'd be no fun in racing them – you might as well take up motor racing."

"Yes, but one day, when Red had done badly, because I was feeling suspicious, I had a good look when I went to thank the jockey for trying and to wish him better luck next time. Then I gave the horse a carrot and noticed a slight blemish on his chest from a scratch that had long since healed. It wasn't there before. The next time I saw him run, he won. In the winners' enclosure, I was congratulating his jockey when I noticed that the scar had disappeared. Space Station won the next race. He had the scar."

He opened the car door and reached inside, bringing out his book of roadmaps.

"That's ridiculous! Why would I do anything like what you're suggesting? Every trainer wants all his horses to win."

A voice in the dark said, "Not always!" Johnny stepped into view, followed by Liz. I wondered where Zigzag was but it was not the time to ask.

Major Fox said. "What do you mean?"

"You get better odds after a poor performance or two. I've been following the form of several of your horses, not just Silver. It's clever. You don't have to dope them or do anything to hurt them. The jockeys don't even have to know. As far as they can see, the horse was just off form. But I still don't get how you work it. I mean, how does swapping horses matter? Don't the fast ones win and the slow ones lose always?"

Liz said, "The trick is to enter each horse for the distance or type of race that suits it. When the major enters one in the wrong type of race, it'll lose, whether it's on form or not."

The major locked his car and said, "Well, now. Aren't you three clever! Now what do you intend doing about it? Remember, you've been benefitting as much as I have."

I asked, "Who else knows?"

Major Fox stared at his book of roadmaps as if he hadn't heard before answering, "Brian knows. It was his idea. We had to tell Lord Brecon. My good lady doesn't know. She doesn't worry about the details. She just likes winning. I think some of the jockeys have guessed, but they won't upset the applecart." He looked from one to another of us. "So what now? What are you going to do?"

Johnny looked at me, then at Liz and said, "I think we three need to talk before we do anything. Before we tell the major what we want. Not here, though. Let's meet. Where?"

I said, "How about the farm. There won't be any nosy ears there."

"Yeah! Good idea, but it can't be until after next week, 'cos I've got a couple of gigs coming up. Still, that gives us time to think."

"That's OK. It'll be half term. In fact I'll be taking my sister there so she can ride her pony that week."

Back inside, I rejoined Izzy who asked, "What's up with you? You've been a bit funny all night, but it looks like summat's happened while you were outside. Come to that, what were you up to out there?"

I tried being evasive, but it was not my forte. Finally I told her.

"You bloody fool! What do you wanna put the cat among the pigeons for? If old Foxy's got a way of getting us better odds, what do you wanna mess it up for?"

The Key to a Murder *by John Harvey Murray*

I replied, "It's not honest. It's not fair. Look, I know I've been using err… creativity in claiming grants and loans for projects that exist more on paper than on the ground. But I do intend to pay back the loans eventually and to carry out some, perhaps most, of the repairs and improvements to the farm. Nobody's really being robbed – much. But this racing scam's different. People are losing money because the horse they thought they were betting on wasn't running in the race in question. I wonder how much the bookies are losing as well as the punters."

"You really are still a vicar at heart incha? You can't just rake in the money."

Our relationship deteriorated after that.

I wrestled with my conscience for a few days before going to see my uncle Francis: one of the few people I trusted and respected. I went to evensong on Wednesday evening and afterwards approached my uncle who was astonished at my suddenly renewed enthusiasm for worship. I walked with him from the cathedral to his house and explained my problem, ending by asking whether I should report the scam to the Jockey Club.

"I can see why you're reluctant to make a huge amount of trouble where some innocent people might get blamed or else you might not have enough evidence to prove your case and end up making a fool of yourself as well as making a lot of enemies. I know. I've been in that position."

"When?"

He sighed. "When you were a toddler, I was an army chaplain. I served in Afghanistan. I got to knowing about a scam some of the men were involved in, ripping off the army and local people. I confronted the ringleaders and said I'd keep quiet if they'd give up their racket. If not, I'd go to the redcaps – that's the military police, who wear red caps."

"I suppose that's one way out."

"Knowing you, you wouldn't be any happier than I would to just turn a blind eye."

We had reached his front door. He said, "My wife's expecting visitors and I think they've arrived. Hang on." He opened the front door and called out, "I'm giving Matthew a lift to his flat. I won't be long."

On the way around the house to his parking space, he asked, "Do you think the trainer would listen or is he the vindictive type? Is he linked to organised crime?"

"I think Major Fox is linked only to the syndicate that he runs. I don't think it goes beyond them. He always seems pleasant, but I've never threatened to ruin a scam before."

"Major Fox? Not Roger Fox?"

"Yes. Why?"

Francis laughed as he pressed his key fob to unlock the car. "I knew him, years ago. He was one of the men involved in the racket I told you about in the army. At it again, is he? I'm not surprised. I don't think he's vindictive. I expect he'll just cut his losses. By the way, he was never a major: just a sergeant-major. He was always pretentious."

"That's a relief. Was he in the intelligence corps?"

"Yes. Oh – he was a good soldier. Patriotic. You could rely on him to do his duty. He just tried to feather his nest. I don't think he saw anything wrong in it."

He concentrated on driving for a minute, as the traffic was heavy at that stage. When it thinned out, he said, "Listen, Matt, I can't tell you what to do. You're old enough and intelligent enough to make your own decisions, but I wish you'd get out of the racing business. I know there are plenty of honest people involved in it, but there are a lot of the other kind. Wherever a lot of money changes hands it attracts the worst kind of person."

"Do you think that's what I'll become?"

"I don't know. You're not one now, but I'd rather you weren't putting yourself in harm's way. I mean temptation as well as the risk of upsetting some nasty people. There are lots of other ways of making a good living. If the Church is not for you, OK. I think management studies could be useful if you start your own business or if you work for someone else. Just try to pick something ethical. I'm sure you can find something and succeed in it."

"That reminds me of something someone said a little while ago. Do you know about the two views of history?"

"Which ones?"

I told him of my conversation with Izzy. He said, "There's a third. The Christian view."

"I must have heard of it. My history masters were mostly Christians."

"God is sovereign over the way things turn out but he uses people to put his plans into practice. There's a debate about how much free will everyone has, but it doesn't change the overall argument. Great men are made by God. You can see it in the stories in the Bible and in the lives of saints, including modern ones. And I have confidence that God will show you the right thing to do about the scam and about your future. I've known you a long time."

I was touched by his confidence and grateful for his advice. I was still chuckling at the thought of Major Fox being a sergeant-major, when I got into the flat, where a letter was waiting for me. The address on the envelope was printed as was the single sheet of plain computer paper inside.

MIND YOUR OWN BUSINESS

Well, it was succinct. I wondered if it was from someone concerned at my probing my father's death or someone connected with the racing scam. Should I go to the police? Should I tell Esso? Not him. His father might be the one who sent it. I decided to continue as planned but be alert for anyone taking things further.

Chapter 13

I hired a car in Cardiff on the Saturday of half term and collected Jan from her school outside Gloucester. We spent the rest of the weekend with Mother in Amesbury. It felt strange going to church to see the new rector conduct the service in a style very different from that of my father or Arnie. By Monday, Mother was glad I was taking Jan away for the week to allow her to get on with lots of things without interruption. Jan was pleased too.

We arrived at the farm on Monday lunchtime, and helped Arnie and Ruth mucking out, having turned the horses out to graze. I told them I needed to speak with Johnny and Liz alone when they arrived, which could be soon, as we had encountered more traffic than I had expected. Arnie asked, "Are they bringing a horse?" I looked where he was looking. Johnny's white Alfa Romeo was pulling into the yard, followed by a horse-trailer towed by a familiar-looking four-by-four. Liz got out and accompanied Johnny as he strode up to me.

I was trying to phrase the obvious question when Johnny answered it. "We've brought Silver because I've told Foxy he can forget doing business of any sort with me while he's running the scam. If it ever gets out and people connect me with it, my image will take a dive like an elephant jumping off a cliff. Look, I'll pay you for looking after Silver until I find another trainer."

Liz said, "I've had a right bust-up with my aristocratic, noble, pillar-of-society father. He tried to tell me he didn't know about it. He must think I can't tell when he's lying. In the end he changed his tune and tried to convince me it was OK because we were only ripping off bookies. I said what about the punters who lose money because of it and he said it's a mug's game if you're a mug! Can I stay here for a week until he cools off? I'll go back to uni after half-term. Perhaps we'll be speaking again by Christmas."

"You're always welcome." I turned to Johnny. "What have you told Zigzag?"

Johnny shrugged. "You can't win 'em all!" After a minute's silence, he added, "Zig thinks I'm a fool. I should stick with Foxy and rake in the money. Stuff that!"

"What on earth are you lot talking about?" Arnie asked. I had not intended to hold the conversation in front of him and Ruth – or Jan - but that's how it happened. I explained.

Before everyone had had time to take in what they had heard, I took a phonecall from Esso. "I'm in Cheltenham, working, and I've asked the boss about trying to improve some of those photos so as to identify that bloke and he says OK. Of course, I should've asked you for the SIM card. Anyhow, can you bring it now?"

"Now?"

"Yeah. Eric says things are slack at the moment but he's off for a few days later in the week so it could be now or never, depending on how busy we are when he gets back."

"All right. Hang on!" I asked Jan if she had the SIM card.

"Sure. It's at home with all the bits of Dad's camera."

I told Esso. He called me back having spoken again to his boss. "It'll be OK if you can bring the thing tomorrow. Eric's not off until Thursday."

Jan and I told Johnny and Liz what was so urgent about getting a photo enlarged, while we unloaded Silver and made him comfortable in a stable. Then I reminded Johnny why we were meeting. He repeated what he had said earlier before saying, "I can't think what to do next. I mean, should we go to the Jockey Club and get everyone in the syndicate into big trouble or just pull out ourselves?"

I said, "What if we told the major to stop now or we will go to the Jockey Club?"

"Yeah! Not bad. I suppose we ought to go together to put more pressure on him."

"Thanks. I'd be a bit nervous giving him an ultimatum by myself."

Liz said, "I want to be there too. Whatever my father says, I'm not riding for a dodgy trainer."

Johnny left us to go to a meeting with someone in the music industry. Liz set out for a quiet ride on Silver when he had rested enough, accompanied by Jan on Bess. I helped with chores, until a Range-Rover came into the yard and Lord Brecon stepped out wearing riding kit. I said, "Liz is out riding. She won't be long."

"All right. But I need to speak with you anyway. It's a nice day. Let's go for a ride."

He rode his old hunter and I rode the cob. As we rode at a steady walk, he said, "You know what I want to talk about, I suppose?"

"The racing scam I've discovered?"

"I think 'scam' is a bit strong and I think you've got a suspicion. I doubt that you've really discovered anything definite."

I told him what I had observed and what I had deduced. By then we had reached a track where we could trot for a while. When we returned to a walk, Lord Brecon said. "It was a mistake to encourage you to buy the farm where the syndicate's horses go for their holidays. Of course, you were going to be a 'hands-off' farmer. It was just unfortunate that Foxy found himself in a jam and had to ask you to get more involved at the sharp end."

"OK – so what did you want to say? Just hoping to convince me I was wrong?"

"It was worth a try, but you've obviously thought it all through pretty carefully, as I had feared. However, that was not my only idea. Hmm. Let's have a canter along this field."

I was enjoying the canter, although I was tense with wondering what Lord Brecon's other ideas were, when the sound of a shotgun being fired close to us caused the horses to shy badly. I couldn't blame them, the sound scared me badly enough too. Several crows voiced their disapproval at being disturbed. When we had calmed the horses and they were back to walking quietly, Lord Brecon stood in his stirrups and stared over the hedge at the woods and said, "Damn! I can't see anyone."

"Neither can I but I could make an educated guess that that's my neighbour, Jimmy James. They say he loves shooting and isn't too fussy about what he shoots. On top of that, he's not a very good shot and doesn't always bag what he's aiming at. He's never shot anyone that I know of, but there've been I think there've been some near-misses and he's spooked a few horses. If anyone says anything, he apologises and says he hadn't seen them."

Lord Brecon said, "Obviously, it's not illegal to shoot vermin on your property and nobody minds, as a rule, if you go onto your neighbour's property, but it's usual to let them know. It's also a good idea to keep your eyes peeled to make sure you don't shoot too close to anyone."

As we rode slowly through a muddy patch he said, "That incident brings me to what I wanted to say."

"You're going to shoot me if I don't do what you want?"

"No, you fool! You watch too many gangster movies, I expect. No! That idiot is the sort who behaves unreasonably, whether in the right or not. No give and take. I hope you're not like that. I mean, you're in our syndicate and stand to gain as much as anyone from Foxy's little scheme. What's the point in making a fuss?"

"Is that how Liz sees it?"

"My daughter has many admirable qualities, but sometimes she lets herself get carried away by her emotions, like most women. You must know what I mean. Surely, you and I can see reason and come to some kind of arrangement that suits everyone: you, me, Foxy and the rest of the syndicate?"

"What about the bookies and especially the punters who are misled?"

"Oh, dear! This is going to be difficult. You're sounding like Liz." He chuckled. "You know, she once told me you were the son of parson and were heading for a similar career until recently."

"Yes. That's true."

"That makes sense. I can see you with your collar back to front. You go for the moral high ground, don't you?"

"Is that so bad?"

"You've got to live in the real world. Things aren't the way you've probably heard in church. There again, it's not all cutthroat competition and each one for himself. You know, we members of the syndicate have become a sort of happy family. Well, I knew Foxy back in the army, the Welsh Guards, but the rest we just seemed to find, one way or another. And look at us! We're different in age, class and I don't know what, but we all get along very well. I thought you were going to fit in nicely too. I don't know if anyone's told you, but we all look out for each other and give each other a helping hand where we can. So just bear in mind that if you play your cards right the rest of us could help you in your career. You might like to think whether all this ethical stuff is going to be worthwhile in the long run. I might add that up to now all the others like you, as I do. We could all be such good friends if you don't go and spoil it. Just think about all this before you do anything irreversible, eh? Now, how about another canter?"

When we had finished our ride, Liz came into the yard, followed by Jan, at the end of their ride just in time to see her father departing. When I told her of our conversation, she exploded, "How underhanded is he! Trying to talk you around to his way of thinking behind my back. I hope you aren't going to let him change your mind?"

Jan laughed. Liz said, "What?"

"If your father can talk Matt into changing his mind about a matter of principle, he's a very persuasive man indeed." I was flattered but wondered how realistic my sister's appraisal of me was.

In the morning I was surprised to see that Janice was wearing a dress and high heels. She had put her hair into an arrangement that would not have fitted under a riding hat. She said she didn't want to look like a child if we were going to be meeting people.

I swore loudly when the car wouldn't start. No way. The battery must have been flat. The others gathered around as I slammed the car door. When I told them why, Liz said, "I could take you. There's a few things I could do if you don't mind if we make a few stops."

"No worries. Whatever you want."

She turned to Arnie and Ruth and asked, "Would you two be OK looking after Silver as well as the other horses?"

Ruth said, "Why not? He's never any trouble."

The Key to a Murder *by John Harvey Murray*

Janice sat in the front and navigated, in between chatting with Liz about horses, zoology and lots more. Liz said the satnav would be an irritation when she was enjoying a conversation, especially as she would need directing only occasionally. I sat in the back and enjoyed the scenery.

We went first to Salisbury, where I collected the new battery before we went to Mother's new home in Amesbury, where Jan found the sim card and Mother insisted on giving us all lunch. It was a nice lunch, but it seemed to take a long time.

I asked Mother if she was sure nobody had come into the church on that morning when Father had been killed.

"I don't know for sure. I wasn't there all the time. I think the only one who was was Mrs Wilson, the verger."

Eventually, Liz came with me and Janice when we went to see Mrs Wilson. She was in the church, as usual. She said, "It's lovely to see you two again. My – hasn't Janice grown since I last saw her at Christmas. I must have missed you when you were home at Easter. And who's this other young lady?" I introduced Liz and said I wanted to show her around the church.

Mrs Wilson insisted on accompanying us and ended the tour by taking us up to the belfry, which had not been used for a long time due to the lack of bellringers. Liz asked, "What's that cupboard for?"

"Oh, it's where the bellringers used to hang their coats. I expect it's empty now." She opened it to confirm her expectation. She finally took us to the top of the tower.

The Key to a Murder *by John Harvey Murray*

The view was beautiful, although it brought back some sad memories. As we looked, I asked, "You know the day my father was killed, you were in the church all morning, weren't you?"

"Yes. I opened up at nine and never left until I went out to investigate a noise that turned out to be your father falling."

"Could anyone have come in, apart from the people we know about, who stayed in your sight all the time? And Father, of course, when he came in."

"I went through all this with the police. So did the others who were here. Don't you go asking them all over again. Some of them were quite put out. They thought the police were suspecting them."

"No. I don't want to upset anyone. I just want to be clear in my own mind about everything. So does Jan."

"All right. The only visitors we had that day were a foreign couple who must have been tourists. They wanted to look around. They said they'd heard about this church and thought it was fascinating."

"I didn't know about them."

"Well, it hardly matters. They came in quite early. It can't have been more than half past nine. And they went out again before your father came in. He was late that morning because he had to visit a few people. It was nearly eleven when he came in. So those two had been gone for ages and they never went up the tower, except just to the belfry and back. I know because I showed them."

"Did you show them out after that?"

"No. I left them wandering around while I went into the office at the foot of the tower. I could hear them chatting in some foreign language. When they left, they were polite enough to look in and thank me. A minute later, I heard the big front door shut with a bang, as it tends to. I told the police, as I said, but they weren't interested. Apart from anything else, why would they have wanted to kill your father? It sounded as if they hadn't been in the country for five minutes. Not long enough to have acquired a grudge."

"No. Quite. Well thank you for clarifying that, and of course for the guided tour. There were bits even I didn't know about the church."

Liz said, "Yes, thank you. You've been so kind."

As we walked back to the car, I said to Jan, "I'm glad you were polite. I could tell Mrs Wilson was getting on your nerves."

"I hope she didn't realise. It's just that I get sick of people treating me like a child. I suppose it's because I'm small for my age."

"I know. I used to get the same treatment, probably because I'm small too. That's why I used to try to grow a beard in the school holidays, to look grown up."

"I think that beard suits you. What I like about you is that you treat me as an equal. So does Liz – and the Armstrongs. Remember when you let me ride one of the big horses?"

"I did express misgivings."

"Yes. But you and Liz discussed it with me like rational people. Some grownups would have talked to each other as if I wasn't there and told me what they had decided."

We got to the car and I said, "When we were in the church, I think you two were thinking the same as me."

Jan said, "What? That one of those foreigners could have stayed behind and hidden in that cupboard in the belfry?"

"Yes. The police probably didn't explore that possibility at first because they thought my father's death was an accident. Then when they thought it was Arnie, they didn't think of any other possibility. Of course, most people would agree with Mrs Wilson that those foreigners couldn't have had a motive, but they haven't seen those photos. I wonder what that man had to hide."

"I hope Esso's boss is clever enough to get a clear enough picture to identify him."

Liz was about to start the car, when I stared across the road.

"What's up?" asked Liz.

"That woman over there. She's Karen Roberts, the one who made the complaint that got Arnie suspended."

"Staring at her won't do any good. Are you thinking of talking to her?"

"I'd like a chance to question her. I'm sure the authorities just swallowed everything she said. But I can't think how to go about it. Now she's gone into that café."

Liz said, "Want me to have a go?"

"You don't know anything about it."

"That's my advantage. Just come with me into the café and pretend to argue and walk out in a huff. Think you can manage it?"

We left Janice in the car and crossed the road. In the café, Liz turned on me and said, "Don't lie! I know. Just get away from me!"

I left and joined Janice. After a short while, Liz came back giggling. She played a recording on her phone. The quality was good. It was a good quality phone.

It began with Liz's voice, "Men! They're all the same. Even the nice ones. Would you believe that bloke says he wants to be a vicar. He's promised to keep off other women and what does he do? Gets off with the first one he meets as soon as my back's turned. He must think I'm naïve! Oh, sorry, love, didn't mean to bother you with my problems."

"I know what you mean. My old man's as bad. I thought I'd teach him a lesson a bit back. You know, show him two can play at that game. Well the one I picked on was the local curate. He wasn't bad looking. A lot of women fancied him, even though he'd only got one arm. Nice man I thought. But his wife! Right stuck up, holier-than-thou sort. Proper do-gooder, you know? Thought her husband was wonderful she did. I thought I'll show you. I'll bet he's no different from the rest of them."

"Good for you! That's what I'd have done."

"Yeah, but it didn't quite work like it was supposed to. I asked to see him about summat and then when we were alone I gave him the come-on, you know? What does he do? Nothing!"

"What? Didn't he fancy you?"

"Dunno. At first, I thought he was just a bit slow on the uptake, you know, a bit out of practice, maybe. So I tried again only a bit more obvious, if you know what I mean?"

At this point, Liz paused the playback and said, "She gave me a wink, a smile and shook her tits. Nothing subtle."

She pressed play again. Her voice sounded next. "I'll bet that got him going."

"You'd have thought so, wouldn't you? No way! He apologised and said he had to go. Yeah – apologised for what? For not going for it? What a let down. I felt so humiliated. I thought if that stuck-up cow knew, she'd have had a right laugh at my expense. Of course, she doesn't know, does she?"

"I wouldn't think he'd tell her."

"No. Course not."

That was the end of the recording. I said, "Could you make a copy of that and give it to me? I'd like to play it to the archdeacon."

"That's the idea."

She e-mailed me a copy at once. Then I saw Karen cross the road and I had another idea. I caught up with Keren as she came out of a shop.

I said, "Oh, Karen! Glad to see you. I wanted a word." For a moment she didn't recognise me. When she did, she looked puzzled but sat opposite me. I said, "I want you to listen to something. It's on my phone. You might not want anyone else to hear it." She looked even more puzzled but came me and went into Queen Elizabeth Gardens, where we found a seat with a nice view of the river. I played her the recording Liz had made of their conversation.

"How did you get this? Was that bitch a friend of yours? What and you're both pals with that curate? Bastards!" She glanced around. "All right – what do you want? Money? I ain't got much. No. I'll bet I know what you want. Men!" She made the last sound like a four-letter word. "Where? Not here – but my place ain't far - mind you, there's nobody about at the moment." She pursed her lips and pressed her body against mine.

"No. You're wrong. What I want is for you to withdraw your complaint. Unless you want me to play this to the bishop and perhaps a few other people."

"How can I? Admit it was all lies? Strewth! My old man would kill me if he knew what really happened."

"That's your problem. Make up another lot of lies if you want. I hear it's what you're good at. Say it was a mistake or whatever you like. Just get Arnie off the hook."

"You blokes really stick together, don't you?"

I said, "I'll be going now, but remember I'll be sharing this recording with the diocese pretty soon. You'd better get your version in first – whatever it is."

Karen made a rude gesture as she turned away.

Chapter 14

I phoned Esso to say we were going to be late but would get there before the end of the day. He assured us he and his boss would wait a little even after half past five if we weren't there by then.

At Cheltenham, we found the office easily enough in a long Regency building now split into various units, of which the office in question was one of the smallest. Having found it, it took ages to find anywhere to park. When we reached Esso it was after five. He said, "My boss is expecting you. Come on."

He took us to see his boss, Eric Richards. He was only a little older than myself. He didn't have a beard but looked as if he needed a shave. He was not much taller than me but was overweight He wore a striped shirt with one sleeve rolled up. At the end of the other, was a cuff held by a paperclip.

Eric made us explain why we wanted to know who was in the photos, while he examined the sim card. He nodded as I explained. Even as I was still talking, he tried inserting the card into several machines and grunted at the various responses. When I had finished, he said, "There's certainly life in the sim card – obviously – or you wouldn't have got what you have from it. I think I know how to do what we need to but I'll need to ask a favour from a contact in another organisation that we deal with."

He looked at the sim card again before turning to me and saying, "I want you to promise you'll take the refocussed photos to the police and not try to do anything stupid like going after the man yourselves. I don't want to be helping you if you're going to take the law into your own hands, especially if the man in the photo isn't the one who killed your father and I don't want to put you at risk if it turns out you'll be confronting a murderer."

"No worries! We wouldn't know where to start looking for him."

"What if it's someone you recognise?"

"I see. Hmm. OK - I promise I'll go to the police with it anyway."

All we had to do then was go back to the farm. As Liz drove, I phoned Arnie to let him know we were going to be late back, but there was nothing to worry about. He said he and Ruth had managed all right with the horses and had brought them into their stables for the night with no difficulty. They were about to give them their haynets and we need not rush back.

After half an hour, we reached Gloucester. I thought we should have taken the A48 to Chepstow from where we would have had only a short drive north up the A466 which follows the River Wye which forms the Welsh border at that stage. However, Liz seemed to have other ideas. When I said I didn't think we were on the right road. She said we were. She said we were taking a more direct route via Ross on Wye. To be safe, she pulled into a lay-bye and set the satnav.

"Turn round if possible."

We all moaned. We had taken a wrong exit from a roundabout and were heading towards Ledbury. I thought we should carry on to Ledbury and take the main road to Ross from there. Both Liz and the sat nav preferred a more direct route. If only it had been!

It started to rain. In the rain, it was difficult to recognise landmarks. As night fell it became impossible. We could hardly read roadsigns. I began to question the satnav's infallibility. At the next lay-bye, Liz checked it and found she had mistyped the farm's postcode. She set it again. The estimated time it gave us was longer than the whole journey would have taken had we not gone wrong in the first place. We needed petrol. We also needed to eat and go to the toilet. Not in that order. We stopped at a garage with a café. The café was closed. We drove on looking for somewhere to get a meal. The only place we came to in a long time was an inn. I said I'd pay for us all. At reception they asked for a credit card before we could eat. I handed one over. The receptionist pointed out patiently that the card had expired. I looked for my other credit card. It wasn't there. Liz sighed and produced hers.

While we waited to be served, I told the girls about the message I had received telling me to mind my own business. We speculated for a long time as to its author and eventually narrowed it down to: Karen Roberts, her husband, all the racing syndicate and all the church cleaning volunteers. I said, "Your father's one of the syndicate. You can't mean…"

"I don't know. Oh, he wouldn't actually do anything or have anyone do it on his behalf. He's not a gangster. But he might try to put the wind up you. I hope you're not easily scared? You've started this thing and I hope you'll see it through. I'm glad you've not abandoned all your principles just because you've given up becoming a professional godbotherer."

"Does 'this thing' mean exposing the scam or the murder investigation?"

"Both."

"What do you think of Esso's dad? He invented the scam and he seems pretty ruthless."

"Perhaps you should confront him. On the other hand, don't forget there are several others in the syndicate you haven't met because they rarely go to the races. I expect Foxy's warned them what's afoot."

As our food arrived, Jan said, "I know what's afoot."

Liz asked, "What?"

I cringed because I knew the answer but I was not quick enough to intervene as Jan replied, "Twelve inches or about thirty centimetres."

"Shut up!"

As we ate, the weather sounded to have deteriorated. A couple came in, looking as if they had been swimming with their clothes on. We had no idea where we were. When we finished eating, we went to look at a map on the wall in reception. We were on the road to Hereford, further from our destination than we had thought.

I said, "I'm wondering about staying for the night. It's not fair to ask you to drive us a lot further in this weather when you're already tired. Besides, Jan and I are nearly falling asleep already."

The Key to a Murder *by John Harvey Murray*

Janice protested. Liz said, "Fair enough. Let's ask for three rooms. Well two, I suppose."

They had only one room available. A double. We looked at each other. Janice said, "What's the alternative?" Liz and I shrugged. We took the room.

I had assumed that a double room meant a twin room, but there was just one big bed in it. I said, "I think I should sleep on the floor."

The girls said I was being silly. The bed was big enough for three. Just. Jan said, "I'll keep out of the way if you want. I mean, I know you fancy each other."

I said, "I think you're jumping to conclusions. I'm fond of Liz and well, err, yes, I suppose you could say I fancy her, but I don't want to take advantage of this situation and I wouldn't want to come between Liz and Johnny, whatever their relationship really is."

Liz said, "I think there's a right and wrong time for anything. Apart from anything else, I'm totally knackered. Thanks for the effusive compliments, Matt. I can assure you the feeling's more or less mutual. Oh, and Johnny and I are good friends, apart from our business relationship. So you need not worry about that."

We slept in our underwear. Jan lay in the middle.

The next morning, the rain had stopped and we made good time to the farm. I was putting the battery in the car when Esso phoned. "My boss wants to see you again."

"Does this mean you managed to identify the man in the photo?"

"He says he can discuss that when you're together."

"Come on! Stop being so bloody formal! It's me, Matt. I'll go to the meeting as soon as you like, but give me a clue what to expect."

"Look, Matt, you know I'm not one for nitpicking bureaucracy, but in this case, I can see why they want to say nothing by phone or online, only in person."

"They?"

"There's other people want to talk to you."

"Police?"

"No. I can't say who. And don't say anything to anyone until after we meet, OK?"

"It'll have to be."

When I got to Cheltenham, Esso took me to see his boss who took me, but not him, to another office in the same building, where we had to hand over our phones at reception and go through a body-scanner before he took me to a room where he introduced me to 'John Smith', a rather nondescript, middle-aged man with receding hair.

Smith said, "Sorry about all the cloak and dagger stuff, but you can't be too careful. This is GCHQ. We know this room isn't bugged."

I said, "I thought GCHQ was in a huge modern place known as the Doughnut and it's not here just outside the town centre, but in Benhall in the suburbs."

"Mmm, yes. That's true. But GCHQ operates in many parts of this town and many others. We don't want everyone to know everything about us. Now, to business!

Those photos you gave us were dynamite. I'd like to come and see where they were taken."

"That'll be no problem. But what's all this about? Who's the man in the photos?"

"He goes by many names. We know him as Vladimir Sergeiovich Popov. He's a Russian spy. He was one of the so-called diplomats we expelled from this country in response to the Novichok poisoning in Salisbury."

"You mean he was involved?"

"I wish I knew. We don't think he was actually in Salisbury at the time, but we think he had a hand in it somewhere. We didn't know he was back in the country on the date those photos were taken. I wouldn't be at all surprised if he killed your father, or had him killed, if he thought he had taken his photo and there was an outside chance it would get sent to anyone who might recognise him."

I said, "The telephoto lens was broken off the camera, apparently before it went over the edge with Father. I wonder if he was trying to snatch the camera and, when he failed, he thought the fall would smash it to bits and destroy the sim card and hence the evidence."

"I think you're right. Obviously, once he'd shown his hand, he'd have to kill your father and make it look like an accident – or suicide – to keep his whereabouts secret."

"I can take you to the church and up the tower, any time, but does it matter now?"

"If we can see exactly where he was, we might be able to work out what he was up to. As it is, we've got people looking all over the place in case he's still in the UK. Of course, we've tried to see if we can spot anyone else in the photos who might be interesting. There's a woman, but we don't know who she is. There are some other people in one of the photos. We're going to try to enhance it a bit more and see if we can identify anyone else."

"Can I have a copy of the photo – the improved version – in case I recognise her, or if I spot this Russian if comes back?"

"All right. Just be careful how you use it and what you say. Above all, don't try to deal with him yourself. If you see him, give me a ring." He handed me what looked like a business card for a recruitment agency. "You can probably guess that we're more than grateful to you for bringing this to our attention."

"Don't forget my sister, Janice, who got the pictures off the sim card in the first place."

"Clever girl. Nearly as clever as your pal, Sam Hoyle. Perhaps she'd like a job here."

"She's only thirteen and she wants to go into the Church."

"Hmm. Still, give me her details and we'll see about recruiting her."

"Have you recruited Sam?"

"I can't tell you, but we know a lot about him. His stepfather put us onto him."

"Major Fox? He's in horseracing, not spying."

The Key to a Murder *by John Harvey Murray*

"You call him Major. You must know he wasn't always in racing."

"You mean he was in the intelligence corps?"

"Well, he wasn't in the catering corps!"

"Could you come and meet me at the church on Saturday week?" He could.

On Friday, Johnny, Liz and I went to see 'Major' Fox. He chose the venue: a luxury hotel in Cardiff. He was remarkably calm and genial from the start. He ordered teas and coffees for us all and a selection of cakes, saying to Liz, "I know you have to watch your weight for racing, but the little dark ones aren't too heavy with calories and are just as tasty as the rest."

I enjoyed one of the least healthy ones. It was great. Then he said, "I trust you three have come to a joint decision as how you intend to proceed?"

As agreed, Johnny was our initial spokesperson. "Yeah. We want you to give up the scam. Simple. That way, we'll keep our mouths shut."

"Well, you put it most succinctly. I seem to have little choice. I don't think you've any proof, but I don't want my reputation to be ruined by allegations, even unsubstantiated ones, and I'm pretty sure I speak for the rest of the syndicate, including, of course, Lord Brecon." He looked pointedly at Liz who smiled beautifully. "I see not all characteristics are inherited in your family, whereas Matthew Chaplain obviously takes after his father. I never met the man, but I'll bet he was not unlike his brother, Francis, in certain ways. He's as moral and courageous as you seem to be. And no fool."

I asked, "Has he been in touch with you lately?"

"Strangely enough, he has. He reminded me of the days when we served together and all the good and bad things we experienced. He advised me to turn over a new leaf. It's something clergymen often recommend. Well, we'll see how it goes, eh?"

Johnny said, "I hope you realise we will be watching you. Now we know what to look for, we'll spot any more substitution of horses easily enough. And you really wouldn't want us to feel you've made fools of us, would you?"

"My dear boy, you do me such an injustice. I am, after all, a gentleman and my word is my bond. So let me be absolutely clear: I give you my word that I will play everything totally straight from now on." He bit into another slice of cake and savoured it before saying, "Now we've got that out of the way, may I ask if you still intend to let me send horses to your farm when I need to? I hope you have found the remuneration for that satisfactory." I did and it was.

The next Saturday, I showed John Smith around the church and up the tower from where I pointed out the landmarks in my father's photos. He looked first with naked eyes before using his binoculars. "Good God! You can see Porton Down from here and it's right behind where he was."

"I sort of know what Porton Down is. It's a scientific research facility, isn't it? One with links to the military?"

"That's as much as you need to know. It's all classified. The point is – what was our friend up to? No wonder he didn't want to be photographed in front of it. Well, we've not heard of any incidents there around that time, but what if he got up to some mischief without being detected? This is important. Thanks for letting us know, even at this stage. I'll convene a meeting with some of my colleagues as soon as I get back."

He did not stay long after that.

On Sunday morning, after church, I was walking towards the car park when Mrs Wilson, the verger stopped me. "Fancy seeing you in church this morning. I mean, what a coincidence! You'll never guess what."

I chuckled, "Probably not. Will you tell me?"

"Well, you know you were asking if anyone had been here the day your father died? I said there was a couple of foreigners came in and left before he got here? Well, I saw them again only the other day. No - not in church, but in the village. I waved, but they didn't seem to recognise me, not that it matters. I'm pretty sure it was them, although I could've been mistaken, I suppose. They were just like them, though. Fancy them coming back here again. They must like the place."

I took out my phone and showed her the photos.

"I reckon that's them. Where did you take these?"

"Oh, I was just trying out a new camera and took loads of pics. When I saw these, I wondered who the people were. If I see them again, I'll let them have the photos. I don't know why I took them, really."

I phoned John Smith on his mobile. "You know what we were talking about yesterday? Well, someone here has told me they saw a couple of people we talked about. Yes, here in the village, a couple of days ago. What a coincidence, eh?"

He said, "Thanks! I'll send someone down your way to look out for them and see what they're up to."

A week later, Mother said, "I've some terrible news. That nice verger, Mrs Wilson, has died. She had a fall downstairs and broke her neck. I don't know what we'll do without her." Some horrible dark thoughts crossed my mind but I told myself I was getting paranoid. The Russian couple couldn't have known she had seen the photos and anyway she had no idea who they were or that they might have killed my father.

Chapter 15

Not long after my visit home, Arnie phoned and said he was amazed at a letter he had received informing him that the complaint against him had been dropped and his suspension was lifted. It had also said that he would then be free to take up his former curacy. His successor had never actually appeared, for reasons they did not state. However, the new rector had said he would welcome another pair of hands. He had probably not seen the irony in that remark.

I asked, "Would you consider going back?"

"Aye! I think I would like to, for now. I might not stay long, as I'm looking into other types of ministry, as I said. In fact, I've already phoned the rector and agreed to assist this Sunday on a one-off basis, to see how it goes, before anyone makes it official. Your mother's been kind enough to offer us a bed for the night, as our old house is now unfurnished."

"I hope it goes OK, but how will you face all those parishioners?"

"Well, I hope they all accept my innocence regarding both the murder and the sexual assault. Your mother assures me most of them have."

"I was more thinking of it the other way round. I mean, how do you feel about them, knowing a lot of them had believed the worst about you?"

"I suppose it was inevitable that they'd believe what the jury decided and what the Church seemed to be saying. I can't blame them."

I was humbled by his lack of bitterness and self-pity. Perhaps my father and my Uncle Francis were not the only clergymen who were sincere Christians.

Arnie and Ruth stayed at the farm, pending his being formally reappointed to the curacy and their being able to move back into their former home.

I continued my studies.

****

It was almost the end of term when 'Major' Fox phoned. "Could you take one of my horses – well one of the syndicate's really – for a few weeks at the farm? It's Red. He's been off form and the vet reckons it's not serious but he could do with a break. It'd be better for him not to spend his time standing in a stable. A spell on your grass would be ideal."

"OK but have you a lad you could send? I'll be going home for Christmas and as there are no flat-race horses there at the moment, I'd have to get Dai, Lord Brecon's groom, to take him on. And he's already looking after Silver because Johnny hasn't found another trainer yet and he'll be busy with the hunters on Boxing Day. On top of that, the other farm employees have all asked for time off from Christmas to New Year. I'm trying to work out some compromises already."

"Hmm. Tricky. I'll be short-handed myself, what with a couple of lads insisting they've got to go home to Ireland or there'll be Hell to pay. Couldn't you do it yourself, as a favour, just this once?"

"My mother expects me home for Christmas, but I'll see what I can do."

I phoned Mother, wondering how to approach the subject. Before I could get a word in, she said, "I say, can you ever forgive me? Your Uncle Walter and Auntie Maggie have invited us to go there for Christmas. I've said I'd love to but as for you, well, you're old enough to please yourself. I've told Jan she's got to come, of course."

I thanked her and called Arnie. He said, "I was hoping to speak to you. We can move into our new home – our old home actually – any time after New Year. We'll book a removal van as soon as we can."

My next call was from Janice begging to spend the Christmas holidays with me, or almost anyone except Uncle Walter and Aunt Maggie. After several phonecalls we agreed Janice could come to me for a few days as long as she spent Christmas with Uncle Walter and Aunt Maggie and I would have to take her to her school at the start of the new term. That sounded easy until I realised that, when Arnie and Ruth left, I would be the only person looking after the horses, as the major's new groom would not be arriving for another week. After a few more urgent phonecalls, Uncle Francis promised to collect her from the farm and take her to her school for the new term.

The Key to a Murder *by John Harvey Murray*

Therefore, on Christmas Day, I had Arnie and
Ruth for company, apart from the horses. I drove them to
the church in the village and we were back in time to get
the essential chores done.

On Boxing Day I drove home and fetched Janice.
We had a happy time with Arnie and Ruth, as well as the
horses, until the third of January when Francis arrived
hard on the heels of the removal men, early in the morning
while we were giving the horses their light breakfast prior
to turning them out on the grass. The men worked briskly
and efficiently and had gone before mid-morning. Arnie
and Ruth followed in their car, ready to sort everything
out as soon as they got home. Francis and Jan were right
behind them.

I realised I still hadn't turned the horses out to
grass and began walking across the yard, when my phone
rang. Arnie was calling to thank me and to remind me I
was free to keep or dispose of anything of theirs that they
had left behind.

BANG!

A shot rang out. I dropped the phone as I span
around to see where it came from. A man stepped out from
the Dutch barn. I couldn't quite be sure, but I suspected I
knew who it would be as I strained my eyes to see his face.
He was aiming again. I realised that standing still was not
a good idea. I hurled myself at the nearest door and
slammed it behind me just as another shot sounded along
with a thud as if a bullet had hit the door. I was in the
stable block. I was glad I hadn't replaced the old oak door.

A bullet would probably have passed through a modern one made of softer wood.

A voice called, "Come out! You don't expect me to come in after you, do you? I could be walking into an ambush." If only I could set one up! I was unarmed and unprepared. But why should I go outside? Uncle Francis had once said that you should never do what the enemy wants. The voice had a hint of a foreign accent, quite possibly Russian. I tried to think of ways to reply. Then I thought it best to keep quiet. He couldn't know where I was in a big building.

The voice spoke again. "You have been most tiresome, moving around so much. It has taken me much effort to finally track you down. Now we must end this. You have been far too inquisitive. I hoped you would accept that your father's death was an accident. Then that stupid hang-glider interfered. Then I hoped you would accept that the killer was the one-armed pastor. However, you have been persisting. I don't know where you got those photos. I was sure your father's camera was destroyed by the fall along with your father. Well now is the time for all to come to a conclusion. Come out! You cannot stay in there for ever."

I thought if I survived long enough someone would come. Who? The herdsman had gone off to his day-job. The other farmhand had gone off to collect some supplies and would probably be gone all day. His wife was at home with some new flu-like virus that was going around. I looked at Silver's beautiful head, peering at me past his empty haynet. Did Liz say she was coming today?

Suddenly, I hoped nobody would come. I feared this man would kill them too. He probably didn't like witnesses, or 'loose ends' as they say in spy novels. I wished I hadn't dropped my phone. I remembered that Uncle Francis used to say that worrying about a mistake is pointless. You are where you are. Take it from there. There's a time for learning lessons and apportioning blame. Not when bullets are flying.

I wondered if I could make it to the cottage and get my hands on the shotgun. It seemed unlikely, as, whichever way I went, I would eventually have to go past the man with the gun. I went through to the tackroom and looked for a weapon. Brooms, shovels, hoofpicks, brushes, saddles, bridles, halters, buckets, wheelbarrows, a short racing whip and a couple of knives. I examined each knife. Neither was very sharp or long-bladed. They were used mainly for opening sacks or cutting tangled ropes. Besides, what use was a knife against a gun? I tucked one up my sleeve, just in case.

There was a door in the tackroom on the side away from the main yard, leading to a patch of mud and grass next to the muckheap. I could exit that way. And go where? The fields were not far away. Could I run across them to the next farm or into the village? I was fit enough to give the assassin a run for his money, but I could hardly outrun a bullet.

I looked at the horses. Could I ride one of them to safety? It would be difficult to lead a horse through the tackroom, cluttered as it was, and out through the narrow door, but I didn't fancy going out through the main door

– straight into Vladimir. I prayed as I tried to think what else Uncle Francis had told me. I realised that I was talking to God as if to a person. Well, a vague spiritual force wasn't what I needed just then. I knew lots of prayers, but the one that came to mind was simple: "HELP!"

I thought about surprise. Yes – that's a powerful weapon. What could I do to surprise my enemy? Another word came into my mind: distraction. Yes. Uncle Francis used to say it was useful to give the enemy more than one thing to think about.

Red was pacing in his box, anxious to get out onto the grass. Bess was calmer but alert. I thought of something ridiculous. So ridiculous, it would be a surprise. I put Bess's tack on her and led her into the tackroom, where I unbolted the door. I hoped she remembered our racing days. I asked her to stand still as I put a headcollar on Red before leading him to the main door. I prayed he would survive this, but recognised that my survival was paramount. I flung the door open and let him go, giving him a tap on the rump with a whip to ensure he didn't hang around. He didn't! He put in a quick buck and landed in a gallop.

I could hear Red's hooves on the yard and a shout in a foreign language as I ran to the tackroom, mounted Bess and rode out past the muckheap. I had to give her a couple of taps to convince her this was a race, despite the absence of other competitors – at least equine ones. We were at full gallop by the time we went through an open gate into the nearest field. I felt awkward on her back but was thankful that I had ridden in a few draghunts on Space Station. That had got my muscles into something like the right condition.

Thundering hooves sounded. Surely I was not being pursued on horseback? I sighed with relief as Red overtook us.

A voice yelled "STOP!" as if I was going to obey it. We were halfway through the field when a shot sounded. At the far end, the gate to the next field was shut. Ordinarily, I would have either dismounted or opened it from the horse's back, but this was not 'ordinarily'. I spotted a gap in the hedge. It was plugged with timber but the top rail was not much higher than the hurdles we used to jump when we raced. I prayed Bess would remember how it's done. As we came close to the gap, I gave her another slight tap and shouted "Come on!" as I took a handful of her bushy mane. She made a huge effort, cleared the obstacle with her front end and clouted it with her hindlegs, stumbling as she landed, pitching me onto her neck. A little to our left, Red cleared the hedge, hardly breaking stride.

As Bess and I recovered from the jump, I chanced a glance over a shoulder. A figure was running through the field a long way behind us. A Shetland pony is no match for a racehorse, but it's a lot faster than any human, even with a man's weight on its back... well, a small man.

The Herefords were ambling about in the field: not aimlessly but all were heading in the same direction. I guessed they liked the grass at the far end best. I rode Bess in amongst them and slowed her to a walk, as I kept low over her neck. I hoped the cattle would screen us from view. At the far end, I dismounted to open the gate onto the road and shut it just in time to stop Red following. I began leading Bess once I had secured the gate again. When the pony seemed to have got her breath back, I got back into the saddle and rode towards the village. Some of the Herefords were grazing just the other side of the hedge ambling along, almost in step with me and Bess. So was Red.

A car came down the road and slowed down. Bess was never nervous in traffic, but I appreciated the motorist's consideration. The car stopped as soon as it had passed us and a woman got out, staring at me. An awful thought occurred to me. Just in time, I ducked so that the vehicle screened me from her.

PHUT!

She was using a silencer and had come around the end of the car.

I leapt up, using Bess as a step, and dived over the hedge, landing on my side and rolling over. I heard the car's engine roar as it was driven in reverse, presumably heading for the gate. Red came to me with a low neigh, probably expecting a titbit. I grabbed the trailing lead-rope and tried to vault onto his back. I couldn't manage it: he was too tall. Then I had an idea. I led him to a dip in the ground, making him about a foot lower. Then I made a successful vault, just as a female voice let out a cry. The woman appeared to have tried to climb over the gate and had landed badly. She was rolling around screaming and clutching a leg, the gun still in one hand.

The Key to a Murder *by John Harvey Murray*

I kicked Red into a gallop. The steering was a bit erratic, but at least we were moving away from that woman. I jerked the rope and got my mount running along the hedge. A clatter of hooves let me know Bess was trying to keep up with us on the other side. I glanced behind and saw a couple of young Herefords chasing us. They would be an inconvenience to anyone trying to shoot us.

Eventually, we came to another hedge, which Red cleared comfortably. Comfort was not what I felt as I landed on his neck and slid sideways, clinging with both hands and both legs. I struggled to keep my voice level as I said, "Whoa! Steady! Whoa! Stand!" I was as amazed as relieved when he slowed to a walk and then stood. I let my feet drop whilst hanging on with my hands.

I led him along the hedge to the next gate, and peeped over it to see where the woman was. A roaring engine answered that. The car raced right past the gate and disappeared around a bend, taking it on the wrong side of the road. The sound of a crash told me something must have been coming the other way. I wondered if the woman had been hurt badly enough for me to risk going onto the road to get to the village and phone the police. I discarded that idea, as she could easily be capable of shooting me even if she was quite badly hurt. Also, I didn't want to put any innocent person in danger, and there was no police station in the village. I decided to try to get unseen to my car, which was in the farmyard with the key in the ignition, and drive to Newport.

The Key to a Murder *by John Harvey Murray*

Bess came to me and I let her through the gate before setting off across the fields towards the farm, leading both horses. I wondered if Vladimir, or whatever his name was, would still be there or if he had set out to follow his partner in espionage, as I took a circuitous route, keeping behind hedges wherever possible. At the farm, I put the horses in the small enclosure where free-range chickens scratched and pecked.

My car was between me and the buildings. I crept to it, glancing around and looked through the driver's window. The key was there – thank God! Something hit me on top of the head and I blacked out.

Chapter 16

I awoke with a feeling that a blacksmith was working inside my head, and my eyes seemed to be finding it hard to focus. I discovered that I was sitting on a chair at the kitchen table in my cottage with my hands tied together. Arnie was sitting next to me. I couldn't see his one hand but I guessed it was secured somehow. Beyond him sat Uncle Francis whose hands were also out of sight. Opposite us sat the man known as Vladimir Sergeiovich Popov. His gun was on the table in front of him and my shotgun was on his lap. A few cartridges were on the table.

I tried to speak, but the words seemed slurred. Popov spoke. "Good afternoon Mr Chaplain. At last we come face to face. Today you have been most resourceful and very lucky, but now your luck has run out." I wondered why I was still alive since I was in his power. I also wondered why Arnie and Francis were there.

Popov spoke again. "My colleague, Natasha, has not been as fortunate as you. She told me she shot herself in the leg climbing over a gate. Then she said she was going after you in the car. She has not answered her phone since then but you obviously escaped her again."

I sneered, "Forgive me if I don't seem too sympathetic. She was trying to kill me." I decided not to tell him she had had a car crash. His uncertainty would hopefully give us an advantage.

Arnie said, "Och! Come on noo – let's no rejoice in anyone's misfortune, even if they brought on themselves. Let's just be glad you're well – or will be once you recover from that blow to your head."

I wondered why his Scottish accent had become stronger than usual, but decided there were more urgent matters to think about. I said, "I fear my health will soon deteriorate."

Popov smiled. Not a friendly smile. "You are under a misapprehension. Neither I nor Natasha want to kill you if we can help it. We want to talk with you."

"Most people manage that without guns."

"That is doubtless true. However, we need to know how you came to acquire those photographs. I don't think they were all taken from the tower by your father."

Arnie said, "Were they the ones you showed me? Och! I thought this fellow looked a wee bit familiar."

I asked Popov, "Why should I tell you?"

"I was thinking of torturing you until you told me. However, now that your friends have been so good as to join us, I can torture them instead. I think that will bring about a change in your attitude somewhat quicker than the more direct approach. I imagine a one-armed man would regard that limb with particular affection. Would you want to be responsible for anything happening to it?"

Before I could respond, Arnie said, "What on earth is all this aboot? Why does it matter who took the photos? And why do you no want to tell him?"

Francis said, "I think this man killed my brother and is worried because Matthew has found out."

Arnie said, "How can any of us know that?"

I said, "Leave Arnie and Francis out of this. They know nothing. Indeed, I don't know why they're here."

Popov shrugged.

Arnie replied, "You remember that I was talking to you on the phone? Well, I heard a noise like a shot and then a different noise - like something hitting the phone. Then I heard another shot and then someone's voice. It wasnae yours. So I just wanted to see if you were all right. Ruth stopped the car and was aboot to turn round when Francis pulled up behind us asking what was the matter. When I told him, he decided he would drive me here and Ruth would carry on and drop Janice at her school before going on to Amesbury."

I sighed. "Oh, Arnie, I know you and Uncle Francis meant well, but now none of us is going to be all right for long."

The Russian pointed the shotgun at me. "Stop wasting time! Are you going to cooperate or aren't you?"

"If I tell you, will you let *any* of us live?"

The Russian placed the gun on his lap again and hesitated before replying, "Of course. Why should I kill you – any of you?"

"Because you never leave loose ends."

Arnie said with a hint of a chuckle, "Come on, noo, Matt! You've been reading too many spy novels."

Francis said, "Remember that Ian Fleming and John le Carre both worked in intelligence."

I asked, "Who gave you that overdose in prison?"

Arnie shook his head. "It could have been anyone. You dinna mean you think it was connected with whatever this is? But I had no idea aboot any of it. I still dinna get it."

I replied, "Was it not convenient that someone had been convicted of my father's murder and that the police were no longer investigating?" The Russian widened and narrowed his eyes, pressing his lips together.

Arnie said, "But once I was found guilty, what was the point in having me killed?"

I replied, "Once you were dead there was never going to be an appeal which might have sparked another investigation. Your 'suicide' would have been taken as an admission of guilt."

Arnie's eyes opened wide, both literally and metaphorically.

Popov said, "It would have worked, had it not been for your questioning mind and your persistence, Mr Chaplain. You really have been a nuisance."

I said, "I take that as a compliment."

"Indeed it is, Mr Chaplain. Your two friends here are quite naïve by comparison."

Arnie looked shocked, but Francis just shrugged.

I asked, "Why are you holding a shotgun? Isn't that pistol more your style?"

He picked up the pistol and pulled the trigger. Nothing. Not even a click. He smiled coldly again. "The mechanism seems to have jammed. Fortunately, I found this shotgun when I was checking the cupboards for… well, never mind for what."

I said, "Photos? Sim cards?" He glared at me.

Francis said, "If you let me look at that pistol, I might be able to fix it. A lot of people say I'm good at that sort of thing."

"Very funny! You British and your sense of humour! Well, it won't save you now. Anyway, shooting you with a shotgun appeals to me. It could look like an accident. Or perhaps you fell out and shot each other."

Arnie said, "Och! This is ridiculous."

I wondered if anyone would believe the three of us had shot each other with the same gun, but decided that that was not my immediate problem.

Vladimir slapped the table. "Stop playing games! I can kill you quickly or slowly. And I can begin with you or one of your friends. What is it to be?"

I tried to think of something to say or do to postpone whatever it was to be. I wished my headache would abate, as it might have helped if I could think clearly. I had been working the knife from my sleeve into my hand, only to find that I couldn't find a way of holding it that enabled me to cut my bonds. It was not a thing I had practiced.

Francis kicked the table over, causing his chair to topple as he sprang forwards. I wondered how he could have freed himself from his bonds. Our captor fell backwards as the table landed on him. The shotgun fell beside him, whilst the handgun slid off the table in the opposite direction and landed out of anyone's reach. The shotgun cartridges fell to the floor, rolling in all directions. Francis began wrestling with Vladimir, who appeared to have recovered quickly from both the physical and mental shock.

Meanwhile, I had managed to cut Arnie's wrist free before resuming work on my own bonds. I was still struggling with that when Arnie leapt up and grabbed the shotgun, pointing it at the Russian.

Vladimir gasped for breath as he found himself being restrained by Francis but he managed to splutter, "D-don't shoot! Be sensible!"

I called out, "Shoot him if he tries anything. I'm calling the police," as my bonds finally gave way and I got up. "Where's my phone?"

Arnie said, "He's got all our phones in his coat pocket." I moved towards the landline. Vladimir broke free, sending Francis sprawling, and leapt at me. I tried to use the knife, but my enemy soon had me by the wrist and the throat.

Francis called out, "Shoot him Arnie or he'll kill us all!"

Arnie aimed at Popov and said, "Stop! Give up. You cannna win."

I fell, almost unconscious, when Popov slammed me against a wall, holding my own knife to my throat while turning his head to Arnie and sneering. "Now are you going to use that or not?"

By then, Francis was back on his feet, and lurched forwards, falling flat on his face as he stepped on the pistol. He called out, "Either shoot him, Arnie, or give me the gun!"

Arnie shook the shotgun at Popov and demanded, "Tell me what this is aboot!"

There are times for asking questions. That was not one, but Popov was remarkably calm as he answered. "I am suspected of spying – ridiculous, of course – and some of those photos show me and Natasha in the vicinity of a sensitive military and scientific establishment. They could be used as evidence against us and our country. I must deal with anyone who has a copy and above all whoever has the sim card on which they are stored."

Arnie gasped, "That's ridiculous."

I said, "Well, it's too late. The police, MI5 and other intelligence agencies all have copies. GCHQ has the sim card. Your goose is cooked!"

Francis said, as he pushed a chair aside to make room to get up again, "So there's no point in killing him or any of us."

My headache doubled in intensity and all my breath seemed to depart as Popov slammed me against the wall again, saying, "Perhaps. But what if Mr Chaplain is lying? What if he has the only ones and the sim card? It would be foolish of me to let him live, would it not?" He glanced at Arnie. "You have the gun, but you won't use it. I don't think you're capable of killing anyone, even in self-defence. You're weak."

"I'm not weak. I just have Christian principles. I'd rather be killed than kill someone else. I mean it! I'm not afraid to die if that is God's will for me. We all die eventually."

Francis shook his head as he said, "I know you're right, but just do him enough damage to disable him, at least temporarily, before he kills us all."

Popov let go of me. I slumped against the wall as he stepped forwards with a smirk and took the shotgun from Arnie, saying, "I know which of you must die first." I prayed. I wished I had the wit or the strength to do anything else, as he aimed at me.

Arnie stepped forwards. "NO!"

BANG!

We both fell, Arnie landing on top of me. I felt an acute pain in the chest and I could hardly breathe. My headache had never gone away but now it was now world class. Popov aimed at me again as I struggled to push Arnie off me. Francis lunged up from the floor and grabbed Popov's right wrist which he struck against the wall several times. Eventually the gun went off and Francis let out a yell and collapsed, shot in the leg.

Popov dropped the gun and uttered what must have been a Russian curse as he ran out of the back door.

Francis grabbed the shotgun and picked up three cartridges from the floor, asking, "Can you call an ambulance?"

I grunted assent as I felt Arnie's pulse. It was only just discernible.

Francis said, "Right – I've reloaded and I'll go after him." He tried to get up before collapsing as his wounded leg refused to cooperate.

I said, "You'd better make the phonecall – give me the gun!" He held it out and slipped the third cartridge into my hand while I staggered past him in time to see Popov run into the nearest field. I fired at him. I must have jerked the trigger, for both barrels went off. A crow plummeted to the ground. I had never fired any gun before.

I wanted to lie down but forced myself to follow the Russian as I struggled to break the gun before sliding my last cartridge into a barrel. He went through a gate in the drystone wall at the edge of the wood. I tried to control my dizziness as I looked at the ground for tracks while making frequent glances towards the trees. A shout came from somewhere not far away. I wondered if it was a trick but my curiosity impelled me to go towards the sound. I came through the trees to a patch of mud and grass. There was a dip in the ground, steep and slippery on one side. Water had collected at the bottom. Popov lay face down in the water. I approached cautiously, feeling dizzy, trying to keep the gun pointing at him. Then I blacked out again.

Chapter 17

When I regained consciousness, I was in hospital with several tubes attached to me and a mind full of fog and questions. The first visitor I was aware of was John Smith. "Glad you pulled through all right. Sorry we couldn't get to you sooner. You know, they only just saved you. You and your pal both got a lot of lead in your chests. He's worse than you."

I struggled to speak. He paused as I said, "Did, err, did you... c-come to the f-farm?"

"I certainly did."

I stared out of the window. There were lots of clouds in the sky. White or whitish. They didn't look ominous. I asked, "Why?"

"Your sister phoned. I called the police and the ambulance as I drove. Your uncle told me what happened when he came to."

"How is he?"

"He's doing all right, but his leg's a mess. He's at home on painkillers. Good thing he hadn't forgotten everything he learnt in the army. He reckons he nearly took Popov alive. Bad luck, him getting shot."

I supposed that was one way of looking at it. I remembered another question that had been worrying me. "What h-happened to Popov?"

"He drowned in a puddle about four inches deep. It looks as if he had slipped on slimy mud. It's hard to believe, but I saw it for myself and he was hardly cold when I got there."

"What about the woman?"

"She's dead too. Died in a car crash. Ran into a tractor. She'd got a bullet in her leg from her own gun. Driving can't have been easy, especially on narrow, twisty roads like those."

I hoped that meant nobody would be coming after me. One thing I dreaded almost as much as the Russians was the British authorities. What sort of interrogation would I have to go through – and poor Arnie? I asked, "Will there be a... an investigation?"

I stared out of the window again. The clouds seemed to have formed one big cloud.

"Officially, neither of those two was ever here. We expelled them years ago. Nobody's going to say different. Least of all the Russians. So they're officially unidentified since they had phoney ID on them. The police think they were illegal immigrants, which I suppose they were, in a way, and the cause of death is *accidental* in both cases."

"Isn't anyone trying to find out who shot me – and Arnie and Uncle Francis?"

"The police think it was some fool shooting in the woods and you three were just victims of his carelessness. The police visited someone called Jimmy James who denies everything, of course, and there's no way of identifying him, since none of you actually saw him. The police say whether it was him or not, the shock might teach him a lesson."

"Didn't they think it odd that I had the shotgun in my hands?"

"What shotgun? Nobody's found the weapon."

"It was in my hand when I blacked out."

As my head was beginning to clear, these neat explanations seemed incredible to me. Surely the police must have thought something violent had taken place.

John Smith said, "Are you sure?" I nodded and grunted. He said, "Well, someone must've taken it before the police arrived."

"What did they make of the fact that Arnie and Francis were in the cottage? How did anyone shoot them accidentally?"

"They must've crawled back there before passing out."

"Didn't they notice the handgun and the bullets from it in the stable door and wherever else they wound up?"

"They weren't looking for any bullets. Oh, err... what handgun?"

I was breathless and lay back on my pillows. He said, "That's right! Just rest. You'll be fine in due course. Leave everything to the experts. I've briefed your pal, Sam Hoyle, but he can't come to see you because he's not a relative."

I wondered what sort of relative John Smith had claimed to be. Never mind, I thought, as I observed the clouds dispersing again.

Mother and Jan came to see me next. Jan and I could not talk about what happened in front of our mother so we let her do most of the talking. She ended by saying, "Just concentrate on getting better in time to get back to uni next term. And you've got time to think whether you want to do theology or management studies."

I had plenty of time to think. I thought Arnie's faith and sincerity were even greater than I had ever imagined. He would make a good vicar or chaplain or charity worker, if and when he recovered.

Ruth came next. She had been visiting Arnie and slipped past a nurse to get to me. She was ridiculously grateful to me for saving Arnie. I said the boot was really on the other foot.

When they moved me out of intensive care, I was allowed normal visiting and my next visitor was Liz. "I'd have come sooner, but they said you couldn't have visitors. Did they think the excitement would be too much? Speaking of that. I told you making a fast buck was boring. Now you've done something really amazing. Of course, you nearly got yourself killed. Not that I can talk. I've come off a few horses in my time. By the way, I don't know what you did to him, but Red Heat's been back on top form or better lately."

"What have they told you about how I came to be hurt?"

"Officially nothing. I think they'll lock Daddy up if they find out he's told me. He had to, really. I turned up at the farm while the police were tidying up. What a mess! I wondered why Red and Bess were in with the chickens and why the place was a crime scene and you and Arnie were on your way to hospital. So was someone else. So I pestered Daddy and he spilled the beans. He knows someone called John Smith, whom he was with in the army."

"The Welsh Guards?"

"Initially. Later, Daddy went into intelligence. That's when he met John Smith."

I had a coughing fit. When it was over, Liz said, "I now know there's more to you than meets the eye. Which is just as well, since you're such a titch. Don't worry, I won't tell anyone what I know. Even Johnny thinks you got shot accidentally, as if someone mistook you and Arnie – and that other chap - for a bunch of pheasants or something. He thinks the countryside's full of trigger-happy nutters."

"That's the impression my mother's got and I'm not going to tell her. Neither's Jan. By the way, as a zoologist, do you think 'bunch' is the collective noun for pheasants? I often wondered."

"Oh dear! I had hoped your spell in here had improved your sense of humour. You're nearly as bad as your sister."

One of my next visitors was Lord Brecon, accompanied by 'Major' Fox who looked unusually nervous as he said, "I'm sorry. I owe you several apologies. For a start, I sent you that message to mind your own business. Stupid idea. Just hoped to scare you into dropping your opposition to my little system for managing the odds. That was before I discovered you were Francis Chaplain's nephew. Never knew your father, of course, but I'll bet certain things run in the family, like stubbornness, integrity and, of course, courage."

"OK - thanks, but there's no harm done. At least not by either of you. So there's no need to beat yourselves up."

The 'major' said, "No, well, good of you to see it that way, but there's more. I did something stupid that did harm you. It really wasn't intended. Just didn't think."

"What on earth do you mean?"

"A little while ago, just before you were attacked, some fellow approached me at the races at Salisbury and showed me a photo in a magazine of you, me and Johnny Whyte at a meet of the draghounds. The article was mainly about Johnny of course, but it mentioned that you were the son of a clergyman who died in suspicious circumstances, which I didn't know, of course. Anyway, this cove says he's heard you were looking for him and so he wanted to get in touch. Now I realise who he was. Wish I'd kept my big mouth shut. Even told him where to find you. Yes – quite - what a howler! Should have asked a few questions before giving out any answers. Trust me, I'd never have given him the time of day if I'd any idea who he was."

"I can't blame you for that. You had no way of knowing. Besides, there's nothing you can do about it now. At least I'm recovering."

"Yes, and thank God for that! But there is something I can do. It's something Lord Brecon and I have been discussing." He hesitated before asking, "You are going to carry on keeping the farm and taking in some of the horses when I'm resting them?"

"I haven't really thought about it, but what of it?"

"You seemed to get on all right with Red, didn't you?"

"Yes, thanks. He saved my life at one stage."

My visitors looked surprised. After an awkward silence, Lord Brecon nudged his companion, "Get to the point, man!"

"Well, Red's not winning many races nowadays. He was most useful as a substitute for Space. He's got stamina and can jump pretty well, but he's just not fast enough. Above all, he's not got that competitive spirit that Space and the others have got. The syndicate are thinking of parting with him and looking for something better." Lord Brecon grunted his affirmation.

I asked, "What's this got to do with me?"

The trainer replied, "How would you like him? He's a fine hunter. For all I know, he might do OK at show jumping or something. You can have him for a song if you like."

I loved the idea but wasn't sure owning a horse would fit into my rapidly changing plans. However, it would be great if it did. I coughed again and said, "I'm not in very good voice at the moment, but when I am I'll come and sing for you."

Lord Brecon said, "That's the spirit!"

A little while before we were discharged, Arnie and I were allowed to sit together in the hospital grounds looking at a flowerbed in full bloom. He said, "I've heard

I can go back to the priesthood as soon as I'm recovered, but I dinna think I will. I think I'm called to serve God in some other way, maybe helping prisoners, like we talked about. I've been learning about a few charities. What about you?"

"My faith seems stronger now than ever. I think God preserved us both for a purpose. As I know there's more to life than making a quick buck, I'm going to finish my theology course and seek ordination." Arnie was delighted. I stared at the flowers in front of us before saying, "I know Ruth's still looking after the horses on the farm. I'll miss her when she goes away with you. Until then, you're both welcome to the cottage."

"Aye! She loves looking after horses. We both do. And the farm would be an ideal place to recuperate. It's so peaceful."

We both laughed at the irony and set ourselves off coughing. When I could speak, I said, "Well, you're welcome to stay there."

"Och! You've been so generous to us already. And it's you who got my case reopened, because you didnae give up on me."

I thought about the times I had more or less given up on him and felt terrible.

He added, "I'll make sure we repay you, as soon as we can afford it."

"Don't be silly!"

That was the plan, as I went back to Cardiff for the Autumn Term. All was going well until the following March when the country went into lockdown. I spent the rest of that academic year studying remotely. I moved back to the farm, arguing it was my permanent home. There were suddenly six racehorses to look after, as racing was cancelled. Fortunately for me, Ruth and Arnie continued to work for me as grooms, since a job he had been about to start was put on hold.

Plans are good as long as they are flexible.

NOTES

1. All characters, human and equine, are fictitious. Any resemblance to any real individuals is purely coincidental.
2. I do not recommend trying the racing scam described. It would probably not work in practice. The authorities investigate unexpected and unexplained changes in horses' performance. Freeze-marking and DNA testing would reveal substitutions.
3. I can neither confirm nor deny any facts about GCHQ including the existence of photo-enhancing technology such as that used in the story.
4. The opinions of the Church and of theological education, especially in Cardiff University, expressed by Matthew and Arnie are subjective and not necessarily fair.

BOOKS BY JOHN HARVEY MURRAY

Accounting for Murder, Book I, *Double Entry*

When former athlete, Patty Rogers, decides to divorce her unfaithful husband, Ray, she calls on Accountant, Frank Hill, to find Ray's conveniently missing investments. The trail leads from Cardiff to the financial heart of the City of London and to Aberystwyth, where the mystery turns into a murder. The police regard Patty as their one and only suspect. Frank and his teenage daughter, Jane, try to find the real killer, unaware of the dangers they are facing from corrupt accountants, racist thugs, a dog-fighting gang, uncooperative police officers and Ray's mistress, a pop star with many faces and a rock-solid alibi. To see justice done they will need all Frank's investigative skills and Jane's youthful energy. And more.

Accounting for Murder. Book II, *Old Money*

Accountant Frank Hill and his wife, Sian, take minor parts in a horror picture being filmed in a castle in Wales. They try to investigate some strange goings-on amidst rumours of hauntings and buried treasure. Does someone not like the fact that the moviemaker, a Welshman, newly returned with his American wife from success in Hollywood, is looked upon as New Money? The stakes are raised when a murder occurs on the set. Can Frank and Sian survive the strain the new lifestyle puts on their marriage and

The Key to a Murder *by John Harvey Murray*

family as well as the dangers they are in from an unseen enemy?

Accounting for Murder, Book III, *New Money*

Wales is just coming out of Lockdown and Frank Hill is hoping to mix business with pleasure in Pembrokeshire where his daughter, Jane, is working at a riding centre run by a client in need of financial advice. He encounters once again the vain body-builders, Gary Edwards and his son Martin. The youngsters enjoy wild beach-parties, taking no account of social distancing. But it not a virus that kills one of them. Is it a hate crime or part of something bigger? Frank needs the help of all his family as he tries to prevent a miscarriage of justice and catch the real killer, but what kinds of danger will he be drawing to himself and them?

Down, *a cold case in the Winter of Discontent*

An Afro-Caribbean woman asks a semi-retired solicitor in Bristol to investigate the case of her husband: one of the last men in England to be hanged. He has to go outside his comfort zone in several ways as he challenges the police and the legal profession, while he is forced to confront issues in his own past. His digging raises the possibility of a serial killer or killers. It also produces a late-flowering of romance. The story is set against the background of industrial and social unrest: matters the solicitor had never before encountered.

About the Author

John Harvey Murray

After studying economics and accountancy at Bristol University, John worked in local government finance, investigating everything from petty fraud to massive overspends and all kinds of insurance claims. He has worked in North, Mid, and South Wales and the North West of England. He now lives in Warrington, Cheshire. His writing reflects his Christian faith as well as his love of Wales and of animals.

www.johnharveymuray.co.uk

Printed in Great Britain
by Amazon

36976857R00106